Addict No More

A Real Journey
Through Darkness

Tracy Autber

Tracy Autber

Copyright © 2025

All Rights Reserved

Dedication

To my lifelong wife.

One day, you will arrive at heaven's gate to a massive celebration, but also with so many questions looming. How? Why? I often consider those thoughts to only come to one conclusion... Undeniable Love.

Thank you for fighting for our family, our marriage, and for our future. You are an amazing example of inspiration and hope. I am so grateful that I had the blessing of crossing paths with you decades ago. I appreciate and love you so very much!

To Autumn & Amber.

You are by far the best things that I have had a part in creating. The pen name that I have chosen to write this book under is based on the reality that one day, I finally chose you. Without a doubt, you deserved a better Dad for many years of your life. But, I hope that I have grown into a father that you know loves you very much and you are proud to call yours. May both of your lives be blessed beyond measure.

Acknowledgement

There are so many people who have been part of these words and pages, seeing the light of day. Some will be explicitly named in the coming chapters, but others were instrumental in quieter ways. To both groups, I cannot thank you enough.

For those who fought your own battles and have had some type of victory, then cared enough to pull another from the depths of their despair, we are so very grateful.

To the families and friends that have lost someone to the ugliness of addiction, I'm sorry. I also want you to know that you have to heal and forgive yourself for any thought of responsibility in the situation. If you happen to be someone in the grip of someone or something, right now, as you crack these pages, I ask you to actually beg you to fight not just against the substance or person but for you. This is the only day that matters, and today can be beautiful.

Addict No More
A Real Journey Through Darkness

From The Author

To the readers of this book,

I want to personally thank you for not just the purchasing of these pages, but the steps and effort that you are taking to change your life.

I realize that my story is not special or unique to the struggles that a heavy percentage of people are facing globally, every single day, whether we know about it or not.

If you're in the midst of some struggle or addiction of any kind, I want you to know two things. First, you are definitely not alone on this journey. Secondly, I am proud of you for putting up a fight against any habit, person, or substance that is taking you away from being the very beautiful, loveable, and worthy human being that you are.

Feel free to email me directly at TRACY AUTBER C GMAIL

Be Blessed,

Tracy Autber

Tracy Autber

Table of Contents

About the Author

As a husband and father who struggled with alcohol and drugs for over two decades, Tracy Autber made a decision that would ripple powerfully through every facet of his life—a choice to reclaim his story.

His journey is not one of chasing an elusive, idealized existence but rather a testament to the quiet power of perseverance. Through his struggles, Tracy's life can become an example of how we might pass through time without leaving a grand mark yet still find profound meaning in the act of rising, rebuilding, and reaching out.

By seeing the light in his darkest moments and moving steadfastly toward love, Tracy transformed his pain—and the suffering he witnessed in others—into purpose. What began as a personal battle evolved into a mission to guide those wrestling with similar demons, proving that even the most fractured stories can be rewritten with hope.

This timeless autobiography chronicles Tracy's journey to reconnect with his faith, finances, friends, and family—and, above all, with himself. But it is more than a memoir; it is a roadmap for anyone seeking redemption.

Alongside one-on-one mentorship, Tracy channeled his resolve into founding the nonprofit *Let's Go Recovery*, an organization dedicated to helping men, women, and families heal from addiction in all its forms. Through raw honesty and relentless compassion, he continues to inspire others to turn their wounds into wisdom and their trials into triumphs.

Foreword by Jay Feely

A Personal Reflection on Tracy's Journey

It is surreal to be reading and sharing *Addict No More*, a story I know intimately through my relationship and first-hand experiences with Tracy. The transformation I witnessed in him could only have been achieved with the help of the Almighty. The beauty of this book lies not only in how it has reshaped his life and the lives of his family, but in how it has touched countless others on their path to recovery.

I have personally seen Tracy's testimony in action—watched the joy return to his voice and the light reappear in his eyes as he shares the story of his recovery. The ability to help others has been a salve to his soul.

Tracy hasn't merely written about the ideas and struggles captured in these pages; I have seen him live them. The rawness and authenticity that flow through his words are both captivating and endearing. Few are willing to lay bare the darkest parts of their lives in the hope of helping someone else, but Tracy does so with courage and grace.

Having witnessed both the "before" and the "after" portrayed in this powerful book, I can say with absolute conviction: if you, a loved one, or anyone you know has struggled with addiction, *Addict No More* is for you.

I want to express my heartfelt gratitude to my friend Tracy for these thoughtful chapters. They not only chronicle his own journey but reflect the stories of countless others you will meet in the pages ahead.

Written by Mr. Jay Feely,
Former NFL Kicker,
CBS Sports Analyst,
US Congress Candidate.

Introduction

It doesn't begin with a typical first chapter or an easy transition—it starts with *The End*. This is intentional, mirroring the nature of addiction and recovery itself. For many of us, the "end" of addiction is not a final closing but the beginning of something new. The end of addiction is the start of a lifelong journey—one of rediscovering ourselves, reclaiming what was lost, and rebuilding a life grounded in purpose, connection, and freedom.

When people hear the word addiction, they often think of substances—alcohol, drugs, cigarettes. However, addiction is not limited to substances. It manifests in behaviors—food, pornography, gambling, work, toxic relationships, and the relentless pursuit of money and status. Addiction is deeply personal, varied, and intertwined with our emotions. It often arises as a response to anxiety, fear, or pain. The thing we reach for in those moments of distress can define our addiction.

For me, it was vodka and cocaine. For others, it may take time to recognize or even uncover. Addiction often hides in the shadows of our lives, neatly tucked away until it spills into view, demanding attention.

This book is my story—a journey through struggles, setbacks, and hard-won lessons. It is not a step-by-step guide to recovery but rather a reflection of pivotal moments that shaped my path. Recovery is rarely linear. It is messy, confusing, and often surprising. That's why this book is structured around transformative moments rather than strict chronology. Each chapter represents a turning point, an insight, or a lesson that catalyzed my growth.

One of the biggest revelations in my journey was understanding addiction as a state of disconnection. Many of us initially approach recovery, thinking of addiction purely as a dependence to be conquered. But the deeper I explored its nature, the more I realized addiction wasn't just a habit or condition—it was a response to something missing. There was a part of me that had become profoundly disconnected—from myself, from others, from meaning and direction in life.

Recovery, then, became a process of reconnection. It wasn't just about quitting substances; it was about reclaiming all the parts of myself I had lost along the way. It was about rediscovering who I was beyond the pain, beyond the addiction. My story may not be identical to yours, but I hope that within these pages, you find reflections of your own journey and reminders of your own strength.

Addict No More
A Real Journey Through Darkness

Each chapter stands alone because recovery is an ever-evolving process. There is no single blueprint; there are only moments of clarity that help illuminate the way. My hope is that as you read, you will find words that resonate, stories that remind you that even in the darkest times, growth is happening.

If you have begun your healing journey, may this book be a source of comfort and encouragement. Recovery is not about reaching an endpoint; it is about embracing the journey itself. No matter where you are on your path, healing is possible, and you are not alone.

Welcome to the journey. May these pages bring you hope, wisdom, and the strength to keep moving forward.

Chapter 1
The End: Echoes of Laughter and Love

The room is silent but filled with the sounds of life: the gentle hum of the ventilator, and the soft hiss of the oxygen tank. Outside the room, I hear the faint echo of footsteps in the hall, along with muffled tones of a nurse's voice addressing another patient. The rhythmic beeping of the monitor nearby is steady, an unrelenting metronome marking time. Despite its clinical sterility, the atmosphere is not cold. It is as if the love and warmth of those present in this room have softened the edges of hard surfaces in this hospital, filling the space with something sacred.

A slim wedge of sunlight gets through the blinders and falls faintly on the wall in weird patterns. The streaks of light dance upon the bed, illuminating my hand tightly clasped in hers. My wife's fingers are interlaced with mine, her touch as much a part of me as my heartbeat. Her thumb strums the back of my hand absent-mindedly, a touch to soothe herself, it seemed, as much as me.

It's weird, this quiet. All my life, I've lived at full volume, filling rooms with my voice, my laughter, and even my frustrations. Now, silence has weight. It holds everything: the unsaid words, the unspoken fears, the unbreakable bonds tethering us to one another.

My daughters are here, too, filling the room with their voices, their laughter, their memories. Autumn sits cross-legged at the foot of the bed, her face animated as she recounts a story. Amber leans against the wall, her arms crossed, a smile tugging at her lips. The cadence of their voices rises and falls, weaving a tapestry of moments from my life.

"Remember when Dad thought he could do the kitchen remodel?" Autumn says, shaking her head. "I guarantee sparks were flying, and nothing was up to code."

"Did Grandpa burn the house down?" one asks, a mix of shock and humor.

"Not quite," Autumn replies with a grin. "But it was close."

And in it goes, the room breaks out with laughter – an honest, full, bellyaching sound to drown out the monotony of machinery. For this instance, all thoughts of being inside a hospital fade out and are replaced by the warm snugness of the family, echoed with one thousand shared moments.

The air is cold, as it always is in such places. I can feel the chill creeping through the thin hospital gown, but I say nothing. There is something about the discomfort that feels right, somehow matching the bittersweetness in the air.

"Somebody turn off that damn machine," I think to myself. The beeping is insistent, a reminder of where I am and why we're here.

"As far as the memories go," Autumn began, her voice tinged with nostalgia, "Dad wasn't exactly Mr. Fix-It, was he?"

Autumn grinned and turned to her niece and nephew. "Your Grandpa had a talent for... outsourcing. He always *knew a guy.*"

Amber picked up the thread, her arms crossed as if bracing for her own laughter. "Yeah, but I was trying to figure out if Dad really could fix anything or just had an endless Rolodex of repair guys."

"Well, if he could fix it," Autumn teased, "I guarantee Liquid Nails was involved."

The room burst into laughter, the sound spilling out into the hallway, briefly interrupting the sterile silence of the hospital. My wife, sitting beside me, chuckled softly, her thumb brushing the back of my hand. The warmth of her touch, coupled with the mirth of my daughters, filled the space with a bittersweet sense of home.

One of the grandchildren, wide-eyed and earnest, tilted his head. "How did Grandpa know so many people?"

The question hung in the air for a moment before Nicole, my ever-grounded wife, spoke up softly. "Because your grandfather never met a stranger."

Her words were simple but true, and as they settled into the room, I could see the flicker of emotion on my daughters' faces. Amber wiped a stray tear from her cheek, and Autumn's voice trembled slightly as she replied, "He really didn't. We always had people at the house. He'd throw a party for any reason—sometimes no reason at all."

"Especially if he got to cook," Amber chimed in, her smile growing. "I think Alan, Sonny, Mark, and Clay put up with his cooking for a decade."

"Grandpa cooked?" my granddaughter asked, her tone half incredulous, half amused.

Autumn nodded enthusiastically. "Oh, he did more than cook. Give him brown sugar, bacon, and a smoker, and he was a force of nature."

Nicole's soft chuckle drew the group's attention back to her. "Do you girls remember why he started using the smoker so much?"

Amber and Autumn exchanged puzzled looks before Amber admitted, "Not really."

"It was so he could throw something on, play a round of golf, and still scramble to finish cooking when he got back," Nicole said, her eyes twinkling.

"That tracks," Amber muttered, shaking her head. She turned to her own son. "Your Grandpa loved golf. If he could, he'd pop up right now and take you to the driving range."

The boy's eyes lit up, and he leaned forward eagerly. "Was he as good as the stories he told me?"

"Probably," Autumn admitted. "I don't remember anyone ever saying they could beat him."

Nicole arched an eyebrow. "For as much time and money as he spent on it, he *better* have been." Her dry tone sparked another wave of laughter that echoed warmly through the room.

The conversation shifted naturally, the way it always did in moments like these, touching on memories of old friends, family traditions, and the quirks that made me, me.

Amber changes the subject, her tone dripping with mischief. "Hey, remember those commercials Dad used to do? The ones for the car dealership place?"

Autumn groans, throwing her head back. "Oh no, not the AutoMart commercials!"

"'Be Smart, Shop at AutoMart,'" Amber recites, her voice pitching high in mock enthusiasm.

The room erupts in laughter again. Even my wife, who has probably heard that jingle more times than she can count, chuckles softly.

It's these moments that make up a life, I realize. Not the grand achievements or the perfect photos, but the small, messy, beautiful things. The stories that get told and retold, the quirks that become running jokes, the flaws that somehow make you more lovable.

I find my wife staring at me. Her eyes are soft but searching, as if she's trying to read my thoughts. I give her a small smile, and she squeezes my hand in response.

Now, the sun has moved, casting long shadows in the room. Time here is slippery, less measured by minutes and hours than by waves. It ebbs and flows, carrying with it the weight of all that's been left unsaid.

The monitor beeps on steadily, unconcerned with the beauty of it all. Somewhere beyond the door, life moves along: a nurse wheels a cart down the hall, a voice crackles over the intercom, and the world spins on. But in this room, time is standing still.

And the stories keep coming, one after another, reminders of a life that I have lived. The laughter and the tears, the triumphs and mistakes – they're all here, held in the voices of the people I love most.

And as I lie here, surrounded by their warmth and their memories, I can't help but think: this is what it's all about.

The words and responses have faded and come, like the tides on the beach, punctuated between spurts of laughter to fall silent. My girls are now in their element and narrate stories with plenty of humor and sentiment intertwined together. I lie still, listening to the sound of their voices as memories wash over me.

The conversation meandered, as it often did during family gatherings, when one of the grandchildren chimed in, their voice bright with curiosity, "Grandpa, were you at Mom's wedding?"

The question startled me for a moment. It wasn't that I hadn't thought about that day—far from it—but hearing it framed so simply brought a rush of emotions. I nodded, my smile warm. "Oh, I was there," I said, my voice softening. "It was one of the best days of my life."

The kids leaned in, eager for details, and Autumn jumped in with a grin. "Your grandpa? Oh, he danced like a fool." She winked at me. "And you know how much he loves a microphone, right? He was completely fine until that wedding day. Then, he couldn't even get one line out without his voice shaking."

My humble wife, chuckled at the memory. "He never got nervous talking in front of people, except for that one day. But when it came time for his toast…" She trailed off, her eyes crinkling with affection. "Well, let's just say it was short, sweet, and full of love."

"And tears!" Autumn added, laughing. "Don't forget the tears."

I shook my head, pretending to grumble, though a smile tugged at my lips. "Hey, it's not every day a dad gets to walk his little girl down the aisle."

Amber's wedding was decades behind us now, yet the memories felt as vivid as ever. It had been a day of joy, of love, of promises—and for me, of pride. Walking her down that aisle had been one of the most humbling and beautiful moments of my life.

"Your mom looked so beautiful," I said quietly, my voice dipping. "And so happy."

The grandkids listened intently, their wide eyes reflecting the wonder of a world they could only imagine. Their innocent curiosity brought the memory alive in a way that made my heart swell.

Some moments aren't just memories, but instead, milestones etched into the very fabric of your life, waiting to be revisited and cherished. Amber's wedding was one of those moments—one I knew I'd carry with me until the end of my days.

Amber opened her mouth to respond but stopped as a thought struck her. "Did your mom ever tell you about how Grandpa was at our basketball games?" she asked, glancing at the grandkids with a glint of mischief in her eye.

The kids perked up immediately, curiosity written all over their faces.

"What was he like?" one of them asked eagerly.

Amber leaned forward, her smile turning into a grin. "Let's just say he had...strong opinions about the refs," she said, drawing giggles from the kids and an amused shake of the head from Autumn.

"A strong opinion?" Autumn scoffs. "He got kicked out of the game for yelling at them!"

Children burst out laughing, their giggles very high-pitched and infectious.

"That didn't happen!" one exclaims, turning to me for confirmation.

"Oh, it happened," Amber says, crossing her arms. "Grandpa got so worked up about a bad call, they asked him to leave the courts."

"That's not how I remember it," I mumble under my breath, getting a knowing look from my wife.

And the stories keep on coming, each one a vivid picture of who I was, or at least who I was in their eyes.

It is not just the humorous stories they share; it's the love in every word. They are not laughing at me; they are laughing with me, even when I am not making any noise.

"Your Grandpa," Autumn says, turning to the kids, "wasn't perfect. But he was present. He showed up for every game, every recital, every parent-teacher conference—even when he didn't have a clue what was going on."

Amber nods. "He was loud and stubborn and sometimes embarrassing. But he was there. And that's what mattered."

The words hit me harder than I expected. I've spent so much of my life focused on my flaws, my failures, and the things I didn't do right. But listening to them now, I realize those things aren't as important as I thought they were. What matters is that I was there.

As the conversation winds on, I find myself reflecting on the threads that bind us all together. Family, friends, and shared memories—they're what give life its texture, and its meaning.

The stories being shared aren't just about me; they're about us. About the moments we've built together, the laughter we've shared, and the love that's carried us through.

I close my eyes and let their voices float over me. Every word, every laugh, a memory: threads interlocking, sewing the tapestry of my life.

With their steady hum, the monitors quickly faded into the background and took my thoughts inward, within the moments that defined life. And I stared at each ceiling tile like one would stare at a book – a forgotten book and thought of the "dash." Just the little line etched across every headstone, hanging in between the date we arrive and the date we leave. It is just a common mark, but it represents everything: every victory, every defeat, every fragile beauty of a fully lived life or not.

For years, I had ignored the dash. The addiction swallowed me whole, and I became an observer of my life. I wasn't living; I was merely surviving from drink to drink and one bad decision after another. If you're an addict, time works in strange ways: days go into nights, and weeks go into years. I had become a puppet on strings, dancing to the rhythm of substances that kept me numb and disconnected. The dash between my birth and death had become meaningless, a placeholder for a life wasted.

The dash is deceptively small, but a lifetime of meaning is carried out in it: laughter shared over burnt pancakes on Sunday mornings, arguments that lead to an understanding, and quiet moments of gratitude sneaking up on one when least expected. It is the choices we make, our relationships nurtured, or every moment we show up-albeit difficult.

One of the most difficult things I learned in recovery is that making my dash meaningful wasn't about grand gestures or monumental achievements; it was about small, everyday choices that, over time, added up. It was about choosing to have an honest conversation instead of avoiding it, apologizing when I had been wrong, and showing up for my family even when I felt unworthy of their love. It has been about living within messy, imperfect life rather than escaping into the false comfort of substances.

Success, to me, had long been equated with the external: making money, rising through the ranks in one's career, and impressing others. Recovery made me see it another way: it wasn't about what I did, but rather about how I lived. Was I kind? Was I honest? Did the people in my life feel loved and valued because of me? Those were the questions that now mattered.

We all have a dash, and we are all in the place of molding it. It does not matter where you started or how many times you go down. What matters is that you keep going, trying, and living with intention and purpose. That's the beauty of recovery: it arms you to fight for your dash, to take back your story and make it worth telling.

The room was quiet except for the rhythmic beeping of monitors and the occasional murmur of voices in the hallway. And I could feel the weight of my past leaning into me, as if even the air held memories of every mistake, every regret, every fleeting moment of happiness not held onto. It is in this stillness that the noise of life is made louder, reverberating in my head in flashes of what was and what could have been.

It seems so vividly clear in these final hours and even these fleeting minutes: what a gift life has the opportunity of being. We all get to choose the level at which we participate. At this moment, I realize that the absence of drugs and alcohol in my life has allowed me to play the director, the producer, and the main character in my movie of existence. And that all began on a very important day, January 3, 2021.

Chapter 2
Just Another Monday

The sun rose on the first Monday of 2021, similar to most mundane mornings over the past couple of decades. However, this morning began like a true addict would have it—on the previous Thursday. That's when I loaded up on all the drugs and alcohol I thought I'd need for a long, self-destructive weekend. What made that Thursday different wasn't just the relapse—it was New Year's Eve of 2020. The end of a cursed year and the beginning of whatever came next.

On that New Year's Eve, I made sure I was prepared for the chaos ahead. Half an ounce of cocaine, thirty Xanax bars, twenty-five Adderall pills, a hundred shots of Fireball, a few Percocet pills... and I figured everyone else would bring the vodka, weed, or any other fun prescriptions to keep the party going. I had everything in my bag, ready to go.

The next few days were going to be a blur. With all my narcotics and drinks and plans in tow, I had complete freedom. Businesses were closed for the holiday; there were no responsibilities to keep me grounded, no clock to punch. This was my time. The plan? A few rounds of golf, a party here and there, maybe a casino run, more party… all the while, feeling like I was untouchable.

The next 48 hours were a scramble, a series of Uber rides, and foggy memories. Where was my car? Where was I going? I couldn't even tell you for sure.

Ultimately, January 1st came, which is what most people would call a benign after-New Year's party. Watching college football, maybe some leftover drinks. For me? It became an absolutely chaotic afternoon. I had more in mind than just some casual hangout. When I arrived at my friend's place, I realized they were expecting something much quieter: a couple of bottles of wine and some leftover beer. But I had other plans. I came prepared to escalate the party, to turn it up to eleven, regardless of whether they were on board with that.

We drank, we popped pills, we laughed, we fought. My definition of fun was miles away from their idea of a good time. As the hours passed and I realized that nobody else was matching my intensity, I started feeling the itch to head home. It had been 24, maybe 48 hours since I'd seen the inside of my place. And so, with that, I gathered myself and left, the party trailing behind me, a muddled blur of my own making.

However, Elizabeth—well, she had a different plan in mind. She could see it clearly before I even admitted it to myself. "You shouldn't drive," she said, and at that moment, I knew she was right. The realization hit me like a ton of bricks, but my ego fought it. I wasn't ready to admit how far gone I really was. But she was already steps ahead.

She had a care package waiting for me, tucked away in their guest bedroom—a bag of essentials for when you're too far gone to think straight: water, snacks, a blanket, and a little bit of peace. It wasn't just the typical care package, either. It was the kind of gesture that people don't make unless they care deeply, unless they know you're in a place so deep you need a lifeline.

She looked at me with those steady eyes and implored me to spend the night at their house. For once, I hesitated. This wasn't how I saw my New Year's Day playing out, certainly not how I'd planned my grand run to freedom and excess. But something inside me knew I didn't have much of a choice. I didn't want to stay, didn't want to be forced to confront what I'd become, but I begrudgingly agreed.

That night, I found myself lying in their guest bedroom, staring at a ceiling that felt way too high for comfort. It wasn't the first time I'd slept somewhere I didn't expect to, but this night was different. This one might just have been the original, pivotal moment—the exact turning point—of why you and I are even reading these words today.

But in that moment, Elizabeth was like an angel. I'm not sure how else to describe her— certainly not in any sort of glorified way, but in a way that made me feel seen when I was doing everything I could to hide from the truth. She didn't try to fix me; she didn't offer advice I wasn't ready to hear. She simply asked me to spend the night. No demands. No judgment. Just the gentle guidance I needed to avoid making a decision I wasn't in a place to make.

That night, I didn't get a wink of sleep. I'm not even sure I actually laid my head down. I could feel the drugs running through my veins, each beat of my heart pulsing with a rhythm that felt foreign. Sleep? That wasn't happening. Not with everything that was coursing through my system.

My body was physically exhausted, but my mind was on fire—too much to think about, too much to untangle. I couldn't shut it off. I couldn't even escape it in my sleep.

The next morning, I had a scheduled tee time with a completely different group of friends—friends who would doubtlessly be just as ready to dive into a weekend of excess as I was. I had them pick me up from the house, knowing full well that they were now part of my risk. They would be driving me around to the golf course, and wherever else we might land that day.

We finished up on the course, and I asked if they would mind dropping me back off at the house later in the afternoon, so I could get the party rolling again. It wasn't that they didn't know I was a mess— I just didn't care. The game of golf had a calm atmosphere; they were just part of the day, not the focus. But it didn't matter. After the round, I was dropped back at my car near the house.

When I walked inside, a good friend of mine was there, cleaning up the remnants of yesterday. I wasn't done yet. I wasn't ready to stop. I saw it fit to turn the music up again, crack open another bottle, and keep things moving. But my friends? They weren't on board.

"Let's crank it up!" I said. "Let's have some real fun." They weren't having it. The tension built up as they started to kick me out, telling me I was crossing a line they weren't comfortable with. The fun I had planned was quickly unraveling. "Fine," I said. "I'll leave."

But I knew it wasn't the end, even as I said it. It wasn't just about leaving. It was about figuring out how to keep the train rolling. And that's when Clay—my buddy, the one who had seen it all— pulled me aside. He looked at me and said, "You can't possibly drive." He was right. There was no way I was in any condition to get behind the wheel. But I didn't care. I wanted to keep going.

"We need to find you a place to go," Clay insisted. "This isn't safe. Let's figure something out."

So, we called around—trying to find someone still out there, still ready to keep the party alive. It was a scramble, but it didn't matter. I was determined to keep this ride going, regardless of how out of control it was. I just needed to know where the next stop was.

We found one guy—just one—who was still riding the same buzz I was on. Clay dropped me off at the restaurant where he was, and I kept the party going for a few more hours.

But eventually, even he was done with me. He'd had his fill, and I could see it on his face. So, we left, and I climbed into his car, still high, still hammered, still loud and out of control. I was a mess, but I didn't see it that way. As we were in the car driving home to my house, he started calling all of the friends that would be okay taking me in the condition I was in.

Then, I heard him start making calls. At first, I didn't really pay attention—I figured he was finding someone for me to crash with. Someone who would let me continue the ride without judgment, who I thought would understand that I just wanted to have a good time.

But call after call, I began to realize this wasn't going the way I thought it would.

"No, he's not welcome here."

"Don't bring him to my house."

"I can't have him around my family, around my kids."

With every rejection, my chest tightened. It wasn't just that they were saying no—it was how easily they said it, how final it sounded. These were my people, or at least I thought they were. And one by one, they shut the door on me.

I sat there, my head spinning, my stomach knotting, as he kept calling. And each time, the answer was the same: no.

At that moment, sitting in the car, I didn't just feel rejected. I felt abandoned. I felt unworthy. I felt like that child again, waiting for someone to pick me up, to claim me, to want me. And no one did.

I wouldn't recognize that connection until much later when I started digging into the deeper roots of my pain in recovery work with my sponsor. But that night, I felt it—raw and visceral. The rejection wasn't just about that moment. It was something deeper, something older. It hurt in a way I couldn't put into words at the time.

And though I wouldn't have admitted it then, that moment was a turning point. For the first time, the party wasn't enough to numb the hurt. The loudness of my chaos couldn't drown out the pain of those rejections. I felt small. I felt lost. I felt alone.

That friend of mine managed to get me back to my house late Saturday night—early Sunday morning, technically. He pulled into the driveway, and I stumbled out of the car. The details of that ride are hazy now, but I remember the exhaustion, the heaviness. When he drove off, I barely made it inside before collapsing. The chaos of the weekend had caught up with me, and sleep overtook me like a wave I couldn't fight.

The next thing I remember is waking up to my wife. She was standing over me, glaring—not saying a word, but she didn't have to. The disappointment on her face was enough. It wasn't new; I'd seen it before. But somehow, it stung differently this time. Maybe because it wasn't just disappointment—it was resignation. She wasn't angry in a way that led to yelling or a fight. She was angry in the way that said, *I'm done.*

I couldn't even muster the energy to apologize. What would be the point? She'd heard it too many times already. The words would be empty, just another promise I wouldn't keep.

After the alcohol and drugs had worn off, I did what I always did on Sundays: I put myself together, pieced together the appearance of normalcy, and headed off to church. From the outside, we looked like the happy little family everyone thought we were.

So, we went to church with my daughters in tow and my wife by my side.

But inside, I was hollow, holding myself together with threads of denial and routine.

Church was just another act, another performance, to make it look like I was fine. And for the first time, I heard a request that I realized had validity in my life today. That Sunday, something was different.

It wasn't the sermon itself that struck me, but one question from the pastor. He stood there, speaking to the congregation, but it felt like his words were aimed squarely at me.

"Is there something in your 2020 that doesn't need to be part of your 2021?"

The question hit me like a freight train. I couldn't escape the truth for the first time in a long time. I knew exactly what he was talking about. My addictions. My lies. The damage I had done to myself and everyone around me. I felt exposed, as if the entire church could see through the facade I had so carefully constructed.

He continued: "If there is, we gather here on Monday nights. We have people fighting battles against those things, and they would love to be part of your story."

I sat there, silent, but the words hung in the air long after the service ended.

After church, my wife didn't even look at me as she dropped me off at my car. She was furious, her hands gripping the steering wheel so tightly that her knuckles turned white. When I exited the car, she sped off faster than I'd ever seen her drive. I stood there, watching her taillights disappear down the street, and for the first time, I realized just how far I had fallen.

This wasn't just another fight. This wasn't something we could sweep under the rug. This was the end—of my marriage, of my family, of my life as I knew it. I had crossed a line I couldn't uncross, and I knew it.

I climbed into my car, where it had been sitting untouched for nearly 72 hours. I turned the key, and the engine roared to life. That's when it happened—the moment I now recognize as one of those *God shots*.

The radio turned on, but not to the station I usually listened to. It was tuned to a channel I had never picked, playing music I never sought out.

Somehow, it was on a folk-country station, and the song that was playing pierced straight through me.

It was Johnny Cash, his gravelly voice filling the car. The words were as vivid as they were damning:

"You can run on for a long time,

Run on for a long time,

Run on for a long time,

Sooner or later, God'll cut you down."

I froze. I had no idea how the radio landed on that channel or how that song happened to be playing at that exact moment. But I sat there, staring at the dashboard, as Johnny Cash's voice reverberated in my chest.

The words felt like they were meant for me. Run on for a long time. That's exactly what I'd been doing—running, hiding, pretending. I thought I was getting away with it, fooling everyone. But sooner or later, the truth was going to catch up to me.

I realized I wasn't just running from the people I'd hurt. I was running from myself. And from God.

For years, I'd lived my life as if I was untouchable, invincible. But as I sat listening to that song, I knew deep down that I couldn't run forever. My time was up!

In that moment, I was separated from my friends, my family, my faith, my finances. But for the first time, I recognized that I was separated from myself.

A heavy load of shame and guilt came over me. And it wasn't just because of the prior 3 days; it was because of a lifetime of living a lie. It was because I had painted this picture of beauty, honor, and a *good guy* that was just not true.

***

I drove home, and that day, I got a call from a guy I hadn't spoken to in nearly 20 years. He asked if I would sell him a piece of artificial turf for his house. I own an artificial turf business, so it wasn't a strange request. But what was strange was that I didn't have his number saved on my phone.

The conversation started awkwardly since I didn't realize who I was talking to at first. He, however, definitely knew who I was. As we talked, he sent me a picture of the project area he was working on, and we ended up setting up a time to meet the following day.

On that Monday, I didn't wake up thinking I wasn't going to drink or use drugs. I had no intentions of staying sober. But I somehow made it to this lunch without drinking because I got up a little later and had this appointment to deal with, along with some other things I needed to get done.

To this day, I still don't know why that was. But there I was, sober at lunch. And as soon as I pulled up to the restaurant, I recognized him.

This man wasn't just anyone. He was the same friend who had introduced me to cocaine back in 1996. And on that Monday, in a twist I never saw coming, he would also introduce me to Alcoholics Anonymous in 2021.

We sat down, and when it came time to place our drink orders, I did what I always did: I ordered a vodka mule. It was my go-to drink. Then I asked him if he still drank vodka tonics like he used to.

"No," he said. "I gave that up. My life had gotten a little chaotic."

Out of respect for him, I changed my drink order and decided not to have vodka with that meal.

As we talked, he told me about the life changes he had made over the past seven years. He shared how closely our lives mirrored each other—

both chaotic and reckless. He talked about his daughters, who were a little older than mine, and how he'd made a promise to one of them to stay sober so he could walk her down the aisle.

There was no pressure in what he was saying, but I could feel the weight of his words. He didn't tell me what to do or try to fix me. He just shared his story. And for the first time, I started to wonder if my life could look different, too.

What I didn't know then was that this meeting wasn't random. A mutual friend, Sonny, had called him after seeing me spiral out of control on New Year's Eve. Sonny had told him about my behavior, my marriage crumbling, and the life I was burning to the ground. Sonny's hope was that someone like him—someone I couldn't easily dismiss—might be able to reach me.

He offered me a simple suggestion during that lunch. "Maybe," he said, "there are some things in your life that don't have to stay the way they are."

He told me about a group of men who met early in the morning—at 6 a.m.—to talk about their struggles and find a better way forward. I dismissed it at the time, brushing it off as just another thing people say when they're trying to help. But his words stayed with me, whether I wanted them to or not.

After lunch, my day continued. Normal business activities include sales meetings, bids, and checking in with employees. By some coincidence, or maybe by design, I still didn't drink or use that day. It wasn't planned, but it happened.

Later that afternoon, I got several calls from a friend of mine who had been arrested for a DUI, going 120 plus miles per hour down the freeway. And because of some relationships I had, he suggested that they call me because I know people in the police force.

So the police called me, and I had a conversation with a police officer who ended up knowing how I behaved and actually insulted me, but still, he asked me a question that I had never heard this way before.

He asked, "Is there any chance you're sober enough to come help us clean this up?"

For the first time in a long time, I realized I could actually say yes.

I showed up at the scene of the arrest. My friend's car was about to be towed, and his wife was there, completely shaken. The police released them into my care because, for once, I was sober enough to handle the situation. I drove them home.

Unbelievably, the route home took me past the church where the pastor had asked that question the day before: "Is there something in your 2020 that doesn't need to be part of your 2021?"

I don't know what compelled me, but I pulled into the parking lot. I snuck in through the back door, pulling my hood low and wearing a COVID mask to hide my face. Shame coursed through me, and I didn't want anyone to notice me.

I slipped into the back of the room and sat down. As I looked around, I started to recognize faces. I realized I wasn't alone. There were people in that room battling things I had been too scared to admit about myself.

When the group broke into smaller discussions, I panicked. There was no way I was going to share my story. No chance I was going to tell anyone the deep, dark secrets of my life. I stood up to leave.

Before I could make it out, my phone rang. It was the police officer from earlier.

"Hey, man," he said. "Is there any chance you're still sober and can come pick up your friend? The sergeant has agreed to release him to you."

I stopped in my tracks. The timing was too perfect. Coincidence? Maybe. Or maybe something bigger was at play. Because here I was, the so-called good guy helping out in the situation. But the truth? I was just a scuzzball—a liar making everyone think I was a decent human being.

I knew how to play the part of how to make people believe I was helpful, compassionate, and even responsible. But deep down, I was just a piece of crap who had managed to get away with things for far too long.

I drove down to the police station, picked up my friend, and took him back home. On the way, I gave him a lecture: "I can't believe you're putting me in this position. I can't believe you're doing this." I laid into him, criticizing his choices and his recklessness.

But as the words left my mouth, they ricocheted right back at me.

How are you any better?

How are you such a fake?

Why are you such a liar?

What makes you think you deserve anything from anyone?

Second chances, freedom, grace—how did I still think I was entitled to any of it?

The weight of my hypocrisy hit me hard. Here I was, receiving grace, once again, from people who should have written me off a long time ago.

After I dropped my friend off, the floodgates opened. All the emotions I had been holding back for months—years, really—rushed over me. My veins swelled, and I felt like I couldn't keep pretending.

For the first time, I wasn't willing to deny it anymore. I had a problem.

I picked up the phone and called Ron, the man I'd had lunch with earlier that day. "Hey," I said. My voice cracked, but I pushed forward. "Where is this meeting you go to?"

He gave me the address, and that day – January 3, 2021, I walked through the doors of Alcoholics Anonymous for the first time.

My heart raced, my hands shook, but I was there. I was ready—or as ready as I'd ever be. I sat in that room full of strangers, feeling more exposed than I ever had in my life. And then, when the time came, I stood up and admitted it out loud: "I'm an alcoholic and a drug addict."

The words hung in the air for a moment, and then something happened that I didn't expect. The room broke into applause. People clapped their hands and smiled at me like I had just accomplished something monumental. Those strangers celebrated the fact that I had made it through 24 hours clean and sober. Even though I couldn't understand why it was such a big deal. But to them, it was.

To a room full of people, I didn't even know, it mattered that I had made it this far. At the end of the meeting, I was handed a small chip. A 24-hour chip. I held it in my hand, feeling its weight—heavier than it should have been but lighter than I ever expected. It wasn't just a chip; it was a symbol. A reminder that, for the first time in decades, I had taken a step toward something real.

For the first time, I thought: Maybe I'll finally be free. And the response that I received... Clapping. Smiles. Encouragement. That, too, came from people who didn't know me, didn't owe me anything, and yet they were proud of me. Proud of the fact that I had made it 24 hours without drinking or using.

It was surreal. The same guy who, just a day before, wasn't welcome anywhere, rejected by his own friends, was now being celebrated for a single day of sobriety. The duality of it all was overwhelming.

As I walked out of that room, I felt something shift inside me. Like a 300-pound gorilla had been taken off my back.

Chapter 3
The Shift

On January 4th, 2021, I woke up as a different person. It was the first day in my life that I didn't have to lie to my wife about what time I was coming home.

For the first time in years, I didn't have to dodge her questions about where I'd been, who I was with, or what I was doing. There was no need for excuses, no half-truths, no elaborate stories to cover my tracks.

And while I had always been an out-loud drunk—messy, reckless, and impossible to hide—there were still secrets. There were still things I avoided facing, avoided admitting, even to myself. But that day? I didn't have to run from yesterday.

For the first time, I was okay with what I had done.

On January 3, 2021, I didn't drink. I didn't use substances and other drugs. And I didn't wake up drowning in guilt or regret. My life was different.

It's strange, looking back now, how monumental that single day was. At the time, it didn't feel like a victory. It was just… a day. But in hindsight, it was the first day in years where I wasn't running from myself. The first day, I felt even the smallest spark of hope that life could look different.

It wasn't just that I had stayed clean and sober for 24 hours. It was the realization that, for once, I had nothing to hide. No lies to spin, no damage to undo, no bridges to rebuild. That weight—the weight I had carried for so long—was gone. On January 4, 2021, I woke up differently. I woke up free.

***

For years, my life had been spent wandering the dark alleys of life. And I'm not just talking about literal places—though there were plenty of those, too. Casinos, bars, golf courses that felt more like excuses to drink than places to play, and houses I'd find myself in, surrounded by people who were just as lost as I was. These were the deep, dark alleys of my existence, the places I went to escape myself.

The thing about those alleys is they can look different for everyone. Maybe it's that friend's house where you know nothing good ever happens. Maybe it's that bar you can't stay out of or that habit you keep turning to when life feels too heavy. For me, it was all of it—gambling, drinking, drugs, parties that blurred into one another until I couldn't tell where one ended and the next began.

My alleys weren't just places—they were mindsets. Choices. Cycles I couldn't break. And the deeper I went, the harder it was to find my way out.

That weekend leading up to just another Monday was no different. It was another journey into those alleys. I was high, hammered, bouncing from one scene to the next, pretending like I was having the time of my life. A casino where I was escorted out for being too loud. A golf course where the game got in the way of the party I was throwing for myself. Another bar, another round, another bad decision.

And that's the thing about those alleys—they always promise you an escape, a thrill, a way out of whatever pain or emptiness you're carrying. But they don't tell you the cost. They don't tell you that every time you turn down one of those dark alleys, you lose a piece of yourself.

For me, the cost was everything. My marriage, my relationships, my self-respect—they were all collateral damage in the life I was living. And yet, I kept going back, like a moth, to the flame.

For me, chaos wasn't a holiday event or a special occasion. It wasn't just New Year's Eve or any other "excusable" time to party. It was life. If it wasn't December 31st, it was March 12th. If it wasn't July 4th, it was just September 12th. This wasn't a "one-off" for me. This was my norm.

I always wanted it louder, faster, crazier. No matter what the situation was, I wanted to crank the volume two notches to the right. If everyone else was having a good time, I wanted to make it bigger. More people. More drinks. More drugs. More everything.

That's the escalation I lived for. It wasn't about setting out to cause problems—I didn't wake up thinking, how can I wreck my life today? But my behaviors, my choices, my inability to stop—that was the invitation. And chaos RSVP'd every single time.

That weekend was just another blur in a long string of them. Drugs, booze, gambling—it was all one big swirl of destruction I refused to step out of.

I wasn't just physically exhausted—I was spiritually bankrupt. Dark. Alone. That's the picture I want you to see. Not some tragic, misunderstood anti-hero. Just a mess. A guy so wrapped up in his own destruction that he didn't even realize how far gone he was.

For me, there were no boundaries. No limits. No concern for what might come next. And yet, even in the middle of that destruction, I can see now that God was there. Quietly, subtly, He was stepping in through people and circumstances to keep me alive long enough to reach that first Monday of the new year.

I've since learned a phrase that stuck with me: Good Orderly Direction. It's an acronym for God. Looking back now, I see that Good, Orderly Direction was everywhere, even when I couldn't recognize it.

It was God stepping in when Elizabeth told me to spend the night at their house instead of driving home. It was God putting Clay in the car with me that night, making those phone calls to friends who all said no. It was God who made sure I landed in Ron's presence at just the right moment; the same man who introduced me to drugs in 1996 was now steering me toward sobriety in 2021.

None of those moments felt divine at the time. They felt random, inconvenient, and maybe even frustrating. But looking back now, I see that I wasn't making those decisions myself. I couldn't. My life was too far gone. Too unmanageable.

And yet, the irony of all ironies is that just 24 hours later, I stood in a room full of strangers, admitting that I was an alcoholic and a drug addict, and they clapped for me. They celebrated me. These people didn't know me, didn't owe me anything, and yet they were proud of the fact that I hadn't used or drank in a single day.

That's God, too. Working through people. Giving me the grace I didn't deserve, the direction I couldn't create for myself. Walking out of that room, I held the 24-hour chip in my hand, feeling its weight—small but heavy with meaning.

***

The *shift* didn't happen all at once. It wasn't like I woke up one day, and everything was different. No, the early days were about one thing: abstaining.

Stopping the behaviors that had consumed my life for decades. I wasn't using drugs. I wasn't drinking. That was the start.

This is the time in my journey where I'm gonna say 30 days to maybe 6 months; I went clean!

But just stopping wasn't enough. Removing the chaos didn't automatically bring calm. Taking away the crazy didn't mean I suddenly felt connected. There wasn't some magic serum or fairy dust sprinkled over my life to make it all better. I had to work at it. Every single day, I had to show up.

This chapter of my life—the days, weeks, and months that followed that first meeting—wasn't about healing just yet. It was about survival.

I was getting incrementally better every single day. Every single day that I didn't pick up or didn't drink or didn't use, whatever I was abstaining from, whatever the readers' abstaining from, every day that they don't do that, they're moving closer to who they wanna be. That's because they're seeing the beauty. They're recognizing the benefits in their life that they didn't even know were there: the people, the moments, the opportunities.

The fog began to lift, not all at once, but slowly. And with every day of sobriety, I started to see life through a new lens.

I had spent years in a loop: waking up each day, cleaning up from yesterday, and rushing through the morning to get to the part of the day that mattered to me—when the drinking, the partying, and the chaos could begin. Even when I wasn't drinking, my mind was consumed with thoughts of when and how I could.

But as I started to remove the obsession, I realized something I had been blind to for years: there were more hours in the day. Without drinking and using, my day wasn't controlled by the constant need to chase the next high. I wasn't spending my mornings recovering from the night before or racing through tasks just to carve out time for the party.

For the first time, I had time for my family. For my work. For myself. And all of these things— the people, the occasions, the simple moments—had been there all along. They hadn't changed. I did. I hadn't seen them before, but now I have started to notice everything.

The funny thing is, I didn't stop drinking to become more *loving* or *patient*. That wasn't even on my radar. But it just started happening. It was a byproduct of not drinking. Suddenly, I wasn't as much of a jerk as I was yesterday.

That's the shift—it's not just about not drinking. It's about starting to live.

One of the things that I quickly realized was that I wasn't living and fighting this battle just physically or mentally; there were spiritual problems at my core. For that kind of war, I would need a power greater than myself to claim victory.

Chapter 4
Oh No, Not God

We finished every single meeting in the room of Alcoholics Anonymous with what's called the 11-step prayer or the Saint Francis prayer.

"Lord, make me a channel of thy peace. That where there is hatred, I may bring love. That where there is wrong, I may bring the spirit of forgiveness. That where there is discord, I may bring harmony.

And that where there is error, I may bring truth. That where there is doubt, I may bring faith. That where there is despair, I may bring hope. That where there are shadows, I may bring light. And that where there is sadness, I may bring joy.

Lord, grant that I might seek rather comfort than to be comforted, to understand than to be understood, and to love than to be loved."

This prayer cast a vision for my day that put me on the path of love, kindness, joy, truth, and faith. They were the opposite of what my life was full of.

My life was deceitful, riddled with lies. I spent years telling people I'd be somewhere I had no intention of going or spinning elaborate stories about why things didn't work out the way they expected.

But deep down, I always knew the truth: I had a drink. I got drunk. And I failed my family—again.

We struggle against the desire to change how we feel about ourselves. We drink and use drugs so that we don't have to face life head-on. There's a phrase I use to describe this: *You can never get enough of something that will never be enough.*

No matter how much alcohol or drugs I put in my body, no matter how many times I sat at the slot machine, no matter how many people I sought validation from, no matter how much ice cream I ate—it was never enough. It could never fill the void of not liking who I was.

The moment I started to understand that not putting these substances in my body could set me on a track to being a better human being was the moment things began to shift. My focus stopped being about what not to do and started being about what I was going to do. I began to look forward to the day and its possibilities—joy, happiness, peace.

Drinking and drugging had become my warm blanket, a way to soothe myself in the midst of pain. If I wrapped myself in that cloak of alcohol and drugs, I wouldn't have to feel the hurt of yesterday, today, or tomorrow. I didn't have to feel anything at all.

And here's the truth: whenever you started using these substances—or whatever else you relied on to numb yourself—that's the moment you stopped turning to the world and people around you for the beauty and connection you truly need.

For me, it started with alcohol. I wasn't introduced to drugs until the late 1990s, but I picked up alcohol heavily in 1988. It became the cure for all the feelings I couldn't face. All the ways I felt like I wasn't enough—those feelings of being abandoned, of being a failure, of being the poor kid down the street—were washed away with every drink.

As long as I had enough alcohol in my body, I didn't feel like a loser. I didn't feel like the forgotten kid. Instead, I felt cool. I felt special. Alcohol became the answer to every hurt.

Over time, I began relying on it for everything. Any hurtful relationship, any unkind word, any moment of insecurity—I could sweep it all away just by drinking. And when the alcohol didn't do the trick anymore, I turned to drugs.

But eventually, you realize the substances aren't working. They don't give you what they used to. Maybe you graduate to something stronger, something more addictive, something more potent. But the reality is this: the substances are not the problem.

I am the problem. You are the problem.

I always have been.

The things I tell myself about myself are the problem—not what someone else said about me, not what someone else thinks, not the shortcomings of my life. It's the story I tell myself about who I am.

This was the point in my journey where I started to see it clearly. As I sat in those rooms, I began to understand that the substances were just the surface issue. They were a symptom. The real work was looking at me.

It was time to take a hard, honest look at myself.

This was the point in my journey where I was introduced to God in a completely new way. Not as someone I could turn to only when I was desperate, but as a guiding presence to which I needed to surrender.

One of the most humbling parts of the program was realizing that I was not in control. I'm not running the show. Life isn't a direct compilation of my efforts, nor is it something I can pin entirely on other people. The reality of what's happening around me is far bigger than me, and the only thing I have any control over is how I choose to react to it.

For so long, I blamed other people for the chaos in my life. Someone says something nasty to me, and I'd react angrily, ready to fire back and escalate the situation. But why? Why was I letting their bad day ruin mine?

It wasn't until I began to surrender—to accept that I'm not the director of everyone else's actions—that I started to see a shift.

That prayer I read, the one that says, *"In the midst of where I want to be angry, show love,"* became my guide. I stopped reacting with frustration and started responding with compassion.

If someone snapped at me, I thought, What's really going on here? Maybe their spouse said something unkind that morning. Maybe they're late for work, overwhelmed, stressed out. I started to see that their actions toward me weren't about me at all. They were just a reflection of their own struggles.

So instead of saying, "You're an ***hole. I hate you. I'm never talking to you again," I started saying things like, "Hey, I'm sorry if something's going on at home. Is there anything I can do to help? Can I buy you lunch?"

That's when things began to change. I stopped blaming the world for how I felt, and I started taking responsibility for how I reacted to it.

That prayer says something else: *"Where there are shadows, let me step in as a force of light."* So there are shadows already, but we have to be the light.

I began to live by that. If someone was struggling, I tried to be a source of kindness and encouragement. I didn't do it perfectly—far from it—but I began to approach people differently.

Whatever you think about somebody in your office is probably a product of all of the time you've spent together. And I guarantee there are some bad days, and there are some days when they came in, and they had it up to their eyeballs with their kids and stuff going on at home and, you know, difficulties wherever in their life.

Be a person in the office, for example, who, instead of avoiding a colleague when they seemed upset, would say, "Hey, I don't know what's going on, but is there anything I can do for you? Could I grab you lunch or anything?" These small gestures become the foundation of something bigger.

I started having deeper, more meaningful conversations with people—conversations that weren't just about recovery or staying sober. They were about real things that mattered in their lives.

I'd find myself talking with someone about financial moves that might help their family or a job opportunity that could put food on their table. These are conversations that, before, I would have been too caught up in my own chaos to even notice, let alone participate in.

This shift didn't just change my relationships with others—it changed how I saw the world. I began to understand that the "woe is me" mindset, the frame of mind where you're always the victim, prevents you from seeing the opportunities right in front of you.

When you're stuck in that mindset, nothing feels good enough. Nothing brings joy or satisfaction because you're too busy focusing on how bad you think you have it. I know because I lived that way for years.

But as I surrendered to the idea that I wasn't in control, I found something surprising: freedom. When I stopped trying to control everything around me, I started to notice the beauty of what was already there.

This wasn't just about staying sober. It was about becoming someone better. Someone who could show up for others, who could see the struggles they were going through, and respond with kindness instead of anger.

I stopped trying to fill the void in my life with things that would never be enough—alcohol, drugs, distractions—and started filling it with real, meaningful connections.

And that's when I understood: God was working in me, even when I didn't realize it.

Fast forward to today, and I can honestly say I'm okay with spoiled milk. Not in the sense that I'd drink it—but I recognize it for what it is. It's spoiled. It's time to throw it out, to get rid of the things in my life that don't hold value anymore.

I don't waste my energy asking, "Who left the fridge open? Who ruined my milk?" I don't go down the rabbit hole of blaming others for what's happened in my life. No. Those things weren't done to me. They just happened. Life happens.

Take the stock market, for example. It crashed. People are losing millions, maybe billions of dollars. The world feels like it's on fire financially. And what can I do about it? Honestly, not much. I can't control the global economy. So why would I let that kind of chaos grip me? Why would I yell at my kids over it or carry that stress into my home?

Whether it's the stock market, the president, or whatever else is going on in the world—it doesn't control me like it used to.

I've surrendered to the fact that I was never really in control of much to begin with. That's the point I want to drive home—the idea of surrendering control. Maybe it starts with realizing that mornings used to feel like a never-ending grind: the alarm clock going off, rushing to meetings, feeling stuck in the mundanity of it all. It's that feeling of, *how long do I have to do this? How long do I have to listen to this nonsense?*

But then, one day, the light bulb comes on. You recognize, *Wait a second—I'm not in control. And that's okay.* It's not her fault, or his fault, or anyone else's fault. Things just are the way they are. And that's when surrender happens.

Surrender doesn't mean giving up—it means recognizing that you can't fix everything. What you can do is change how you respond to it. Instead of grabbing a bottle when something bad happens at work or when your team loses the big game, you take a step back. You don't need to drink about it or escape from it.

It's about small steps. Fractional progress. Half a percent better. A quarter percent better. Every single day. You grow a little more, heal a little more. And with that growth, life starts to feel more alive, more awake. You start seeing and hearing things differently. Life takes on new meaning.

It's like that prayer I mentioned—it becomes about peace. It's about asking yourself, *how can I be more peaceful?* Maybe yesterday, I didn't drink. I didn't use it. And on top of that, I was more patient. That's progress. And as you keep going, these little benefits pile up: you're kinder, more loving, more patient.

Here's the visual I have: I think we all have some idea of what God is. Different people call it different things. Einstein called it a "source." Some people say "the universe" or "energy." To me, it's all the same thing. It all comes back to one Creator, one power.

Even Einstein, who never said the word "God," was often talking about God in ways that were deeper than some people in church pews. He was describing the beginning, the end, the fullness of it all—not some guy in the sky.

My Grandma introduced me to her God when I was a kid. Maybe someone in your life did something like that with you. I now understand that her version of God was based on her life experiences, her needs, and her trauma. She came to believe in something that doesn't necessarily suit me today.

Once you can define the character, picture the attributes, or explain the workings, that's not God. He is so much stronger, more powerful, and fuller of love than you could ever imagine.

That's why I say today that I have found a God with whom I can do business. Not my grandma's God, or something I heard about on TV or YouTube, a real power that I can surrender to daily with my worries, frustrations, and difficulties. Now, I don't look for the burning bush moments in my life.

God isn't just in the peaceful hymns of Sunday mornings. God's in the chaos. God's in the ruckus. God's in the noise and mess of life. I just didn't see Him before.

God shows up in a toddler's laughter, a beautiful Arizona sunset, and, most obviously, the voice of the people who have shown up in my life.

Chapter 5
The Power of People

In my active addiction, I was clothed in shame, guilt, depression, and loneliness. Even in the middle of a loud party or an event where the music was thumping, and the room was packed with people, I felt completely and utterly alone.

I now recognize that feeling as a separation from myself. It wasn't just that I was physically surrounded by others but emotionally isolated. The life I was living was disconnected—from others, from my true self, and from the kind of connection I deeply craved.

***

There's a study that came out of the University of California, Berkeley, involving mice. The idea behind it is simple and profound.

They took a single mouse and placed it in a container with two water bottles. One had plain water, and the other was laced with cocaine. Left all alone, the mouse kept going back to the cocaine-laced water, day after day, using it as its sole source of comfort.

But then, they changed the environment. They brought in other mice, activities, and opportunities for the mouse to engage in a community. Almost immediately, the mouse stopped drinking the cocaine-laced water and returned to the plain water instead.

The lesson? When we're left alone with no community, substances—like drugs or alcohol—become a false way to suppress the pain of isolation. But when we're surrounded by connection, purpose, and relationships, the need to numb those feelings disappears.

This is where the saying comes from: *The opposite of addiction isn't sobriety—it's connection.*

Substances give a false sense of security. They mask the emptiness and convince you, even for a little while, that everything is okay.

When I look back, I see how disconnected I was—not just from others but from myself. Addiction thrives in isolation. It feeds on the lies we tell ourselves: You're alone. No one cares. You can't do this.

But connection tells a different story.

Nobody sets out to be an addict or an alcoholic. Drugs and alcohol become a warm blanket to cover the unbearable feelings of being alone.

What I really wanted wasn't the next drink or the next high—I wanted to feel safe. I wanted to feel needed, peaceful, and loved.

As soon as I stopped drinking and partying, the emotions I had been running from started showing up. Some of these feelings had been buried for years—pain, regret, sadness. Others were easier to tap into, especially when I surrounded myself with the right people.

That's when I heard a saying from a friend that stuck with me: "God wears people's clothes."

This is the foundation my recovery is built on: **people**. On the days when I didn't believe I could make it, when I wanted to give up, it was people who carried me. They showed up, spoke truth into my life, and reminded me why I started this journey in the first place.

I also understand now that these people aren't just here to keep me sober. They play instrumental roles in every part of my life. My family, my work, my finances—these people have helped me rebuild and establish every foundation that was crumbling under the weight of my addiction.

They weren't just cheerleaders on the sidelines. They stepped into the mess with me, offering guidance, accountability, and compassion. They weren't perfect, and neither was I, but they were present.

When I leaned into relationships, I realized I wasn't alone. The people in my life helped me see that sobriety wasn't just about not drinking or using—it was about truly living. It was about finding meaning in the everyday moments, about showing up for others and letting them show up for me.

Sobriety didn't remove all my struggles. But with the support of my community, I learned to face life head-on instead of running from it.

I began to have meaningful conversations—about recovery, yes, but also about life. We talked about finances, family, work, and dreams. The kind of conversations that remind you what it means to be human, to be connected.

***

When I had trouble in my marriage, Sonny was the guy I called for Black Rock coffee. If business wasn't going the way I wanted, Alan was always up for a long lunch to talk things through.

Katie became a true friend, someone I could say anything to and get an honest answer. It wasn't always what I wanted to hear, but it was always what I needed.

And then there are men like Blake and Brent, who are constants in my recovery. We laugh, we cry, and most importantly, we attack life together.

Who are those people in your life? The teammate, the man or woman you can absolutely say anything to without fear of judgment, manipulation, or pressure. They are imperative to recovery. For me, it's impossible to overstate the importance of these relationships.

Some things I share with Brent or Katie might make them laugh, while Nicole—my wife—might not find them funny at all. Why? Because those same thoughts or memories pick at old wounds and scars, I created in her life.

That's when I realized something important: it's not reasonable to think that one person can fill every role in your life. Just like the mice in the Berkeley study, we're created for connection. We're created for the community.

Life is multifaceted, and so are we. We need guidance, support, correction, and love—and no single person can provide all of that. When we take the time to identify the people in our lives who are capable of filling those roles, life takes on a new meaning.

Relationships become stronger. Burdens feel lighter because they're shared. The weight of the world doesn't feel so heavy when someone is helping you carry it.

As we build and lean into these connections, our lives begin to transform. We stop living in survival mode and start seeking joy—and we actually find it. We stop focusing on what's missing and begin to see the glass half full.

Life, even with its challenges, becomes something meaningful. We start to see that our time on this earth holds a purpose.

For me, that purpose isn't just about staying sober or avoiding toxic behaviors. Those things are important, of course, but they're not the goal. The goal is recovery.

And recovery is bigger than just abstaining. It's about living fully. It's about connecting deeply. It's about becoming the best version of ourselves, one relationship, one conversation, one moment of connection at a time. In recovery, I learned how to build a network of people I could count on.

During the times of addiction, my life was stagnant. Every day was the same. If I walked into the bar in my hometown, I'd see the same faces, telling the same stories, living the same lives they were 10 or 20 years ago.

That life stopped working for me anymore. I didn't want my life to be like *Cheers*, where nothing changes and everyone stays stuck. I wanted my life to hold weight and to have meaning, and the only way to grow is through connection.

One of the best pieces of advice I ever got came from my friend Brock. He told me, "You need to know who your 3 AM people are."

And this isn't just talking about someone to call when things fall apart—though that's important. It means knowing who you can rely on in every season of life. Who do you call on a bad day? And just as important, who do you call to celebrate a great day?

Building a support system isn't just about surviving; it's about having people who lift you up, challenge you, and grow with you. When I'm surrounded by my "3 AM people," I'm not just staying sober—I'm learning, growing, and becoming the person I was meant to be.

The beauty of this network isn't just what I get from it—it's what I can give back. When I'm connected to others, I have the energy to be there for them. I can celebrate their wins, support their struggles, and offer guidance when they need it.

In addiction, life was all about me—my pain, my numbing, my avoidance. In recovery, life is about what I can give. People are the foundation of recovery, and they're the foundation of a meaningful life. When I'm connected to others, I'm no longer stuck in the same old routine. I'm living a life that matters.

***

In the program of Alcoholics Anonymous, one of the first things they recommend is getting a sponsor. A sponsor's role is to guide you through the 12 steps of recovery, walking alongside you in the process. For me, that person was Ron. We've already introduced him earlier, but it's important to emphasize the vital role he played.

Ron had been down this path before. He had seen his life unravel, felt the chaos, and made the decision to change. His reasons for wanting to stay sober mirrored my own—future weddings, grandchildren, and life experiences with his family. Talking with him helped me understand that recovery isn't something you can do alone. You need someone who has walked a similar path.

Whether you're struggling with alcohol, drugs, food addiction, or anything else, it's crucial to find someone who understands your specific challenges. That's why these groups and communities exist—to connect you with people who can relate to your struggles. Not everyone will be the right fit, and that's okay. I met plenty of people in recovery who weren't on the same path as me or who weren't taking their sobriety as seriously. But I kept showing up, seeking out those who could positively influence my life.

I once heard someone say, "Sometimes, you need to pull over your bus in life and kick people off so you can make room for the right passengers." That stuck with me. I had a lot of passengers on my bus who weren't contributing anything meaningful. They were just there, riding the wave of my life, taking up space. When I realized they had no real value, I stopped the bus, opened the door, and let them off.

The right people—the ones I let on my bus— brought something entirely different. They didn't want anything from me. They didn't manipulate, use, or deceive me. They weren't looking for a free meal, drugs, or a loan. They simply wanted to connect.

For the first time, I found people who just wanted to grab coffee or have lunch because they cared. They showed up for me, not to take from me, but to help me heal. And when I tuned into that, I saw what I now believe to be God working through them. As the saying goes, "God wears people's clothes."

When I spend time with my daughters, my wife, or my recovery family, I can feel God's presence in those moments. These people don't just help me stay sober; they help me rebuild every aspect of my life—my family, my work, and my overall well-being.

What I've learned is that not every day in recovery is a struggle. The longer I stayed sober, the less often I found myself clinging to my chair in a meeting, white-knuckling it through the day. The obsession to drink and use began to fade.

But there were still moments when I needed someone. There were five or six specific days in my first year of sobriety when I truly struggled. In those days, it wasn't just about not drinking—it was about leaning on the people I had put in my life. When tragedy struck, when life got heavy, these friends showed up.

Rather than grabbing a drink, they'd suggest grabbing a coffee. Instead of drowning my emotions, they'd invite me to play pickleball or have a conversation. They weren't just invested in my sobriety—they cared about me as a person.

To anyone struggling to find a support system, I encourage you to keep trying. These people can be found in so many places: in recovery rooms, at the gym, or on a softball field. I know this because when I became vulnerable enough to admit my struggles, I discovered I wasn't alone.

Many of the people I needed were already in my life—acquaintances, coworkers, friends I hadn't leaned on. When I opened up and said, "I'm not okay," those people stepped forward. The vulnerability allowed me to reposition them in vital roles.

For years, I kept my struggles to myself, convinced I had to carry my burdens alone. But the truth is, when you share your struggles, you lighten the load. When I told a friend I was struggling with my daughters, he said, "Yeah, I've been through something like that. Have you tried this?" And because he cared, he'd follow up: "How are things going with your daughters?"

That's the difference between the people I surrounded myself with in addiction and the people in my recovery. In addiction, no one cared about how I was doing or the relationships I was ruining. They only cared about what I could give them.

In recovery, I realized people truly do care. They're out there, and they're ready to connect. You just have to be willing to find them.

Recovery communities exist everywhere, even in places you wouldn't expect. Did you know there's an AA meeting on every cruise ship every single day? I didn't. I thought cruises were just about partying, drinking, and gambling. But somewhere on that ship, there's a room full of people gathering to support each other and say, "I struggle, too."

Sober communities exist for almost anything—softball teams, yoga classes, gyms. I used to think the world revolved around partying. Now, I see that people still love sports, travel, and connection, but they've chosen to engage in those things differently.

When I became that mouse searching for connection, not cocaine, my life got lighter. When I surrounded myself with the right people, I found joy again. I realized I wasn't alone.

75

With that, of course, I want to stay sober. I want to abstain from toxic behaviors. But more than that, I want to recover.

Chapter 6
Recovery VS Sobriety

Oftentimes, the words *recovery* and *sobriety* are used interchangeably. People assume they mean the same thing. However, I've learned that there's a stark contrast between the two. Sobriety is necessary for recovery, but sobriety alone does not ensure recovery.

Sobriety is about abstinence—stopping the use of a substance or behavior. Recovery, on the other hand, is a journey of healing. It's about addressing the reasons I reached for those substances in the first place. Long before I ever put a drink or a drug in my body, I had experienced trauma. I'd been hurt, abandoned, cheated, and abused. Those wounds shaped me, leaving me searching for something—anything—that could numb the pain.

Trauma, by definition, is the feeling I've been trying to suppress, numb, or escape. While sobriety is the act of not putting something in my body to mask those feelings, recovery is the process of facing them head-on and curing them.

When something traumatic happens—whether it's physical, emotional, or psychological—the pain feels overwhelming. For an addict, the instinct is to avoid that pain. To not feel it. And the easiest way to escape is through substances.

Something bad happens, and I reach for a drink. A feeling like anger shows up, and I use drugs to push it down. A few days later, sadness comes along, and I numb it in the same way. Over time, using substances becomes second nature—a reaction so ingrained that I barely recognize it.

Sobriety is about stopping those behaviors. But when you've been using the same coping mechanisms for years—or, in my case, decades—stopping is easier said than done.

That's where 12-step programs like Alcoholics Anonymous, Narcotics Anonymous, or Celebrate Recovery come into play. These programs provide a foundation for stopping the behavior, but they weren't necessarily designed to lead people to full recovery. Oftentimes, they create a space where people gather to "white knuckle" their way through sobriety together, saying, *"Let's just not drink today."*

While that's a good starting point, it isn't sustainable in the long term. Early in my journey, I heard the phrase, *"You have to get comfortable being uncomfortable."* At the time, I thought it made sense.

But looking back, I don't agree with that idea anymore.

If anyone remains uncomfortable for too long, disaster is inevitable. Eventually, we seek relief. And for addicts, that relief is often found in the same substances or behaviors we've used in the past.

Today, I recognize the space between pain and relief as something else entirely: healing.

Visualize this: on one side, there's pain—frustration, anger, fear, sadness. On the other side is relief. Recovery happens in the space between those two points. That space is where healing occurs. It's where I process the hurt instead of running from it.

To enter that space, I have to be substance-free. Clarity is key to identifying what I'm truly running from. Drugs, alcohol, gambling, food, pornography—whatever the addiction is, it clouds the truth. Removing it allows me to ask the real questions:

- Why am I putting this in my body?
- What feelings am I trying to escape?
- What's at the root of my behaviors?

Discovery is crucial in the early stages of sobriety if recovery is the goal. It's about identifying the reasons behind the addiction. For me, it wasn't as simple as wanting to have a good time. When I was honest with myself, I saw the truth: I drank because my week was awful, because I wanted to forget how I felt because I couldn't face my reality.

I sat with questions like these for long periods of time:

- Why do I keep hurting myself and others over things that happened in the past?
- Have I hit rock bottom yet?
- When is enough truly enough?

These questions demanded rigorous honesty from me. I had to enter what I call *the realm of truth.* And while it was uncomfortable, it was necessary.

No matter where you are on this journey, ask yourself the raw, authentic question: *Am I happy with my life today?* If you answer *no* to that question—if you're not happy with where you are—then the next question is: *What are you going to do about it?*

Early in sobriety, there were many days when my answer to that question was *no.* I wasn't happy. My life didn't feel fulfilling or joyful. But I followed that question with another: *What am I willing to change?*

Whether you're three days sober or thirty years sober, that question still matters. If the answer is *no,* ask yourself what steps you'll take to heal. Recovery isn't just about staying sober—it's about addressing the mind, body, and spirit.

Sobriety is the foundation, but recovery is the rebuilding of a life that's meaningful, purposeful, and whole. It's not about white-knuckling through the hard times. It's about doing the hard work to heal so those moments don't control you anymore.

With recovery, I'm no longer avoiding pain. I'm facing it, processing it, and growing stronger because of it. And that, to me, is the difference between simply staying sober and truly recovering.

***

I sat in the cold room of an AA meeting for months, and certain thoughts crept in from time to time. One of them hinged on the idea that I might have to cut certain places and people out of my life forever. I couldn't shake the question: *Was it a complete reset? Would I have to find an entirely new circle of friends?*

I had spent decades with some of those buddies, hanging out in the bars we frequented together. The thought of walking away from it all felt heavy. But as I sat with it, I realized that avoiding every relationship or space where drinking and partying took place didn't have to be the answer. Not every connection in my life had to be predicated on whether or not someone partied like I used to.

With that clarity, I made a call to my friend Frank to let him know I'd be at the event on Saturday with the RTO crowd. His immediate response was, *"Wait, I thought you weren't drinking?"*

It's funny how a place or group of people can become so synonymous with drinking and drugging that showing up sober seems impossible. I assured him that he was correct—I wasn't drinking, and that streak would continue long after Saturday's gathering. But I wasn't completely sure how I'd manage it.

The answer came when I started reevaluating the value I placed on so many activities in my life that had been overshadowed by the chaos of the parties. When I committed to calm dinners, quiet fires, and meaningful conversations with friends and family, the bar began to lose its appeal. I started seeing that I could reclaim spaces that once felt inescapable.

Recovery didn't mean avoiding every place I had ever been. It meant sitting in those same seats I'd occupied for years and knowing I had the power to leave when I wanted.

That Saturday afternoon, I walked into the parking lot with one clear intention: *to be there on my terms.* I would arrive when I wanted and leave in time to be home for the good stuff—the laughter, the moments, the memories I had been missing for so long.

That afternoon gave me something I hadn't felt in a long time: hope. It showed me that change, growth, and recovery were possible. If the *what* and *why* were strong enough, the *how* would take care of itself.

***

Recovery isn't just about stopping the use of drugs or alcohol. It's about healing. And in plenty of cases, healing requires therapy. Just like recovering from a broken bone or surgery often demands physical therapy, emotional and mental injuries require their own forms of treatment.

I've heard countless stories about how people shifted their mindsets and rewired their neurological pathways through practices like cold plunging or EMDR (Eye Movement Desensitization and Reprocessing) therapy. These tools go beyond just abstaining from substances—they help address the root issues because true recovery requires more than simply resisting the subtle foe of addiction.

It's not enough to just stop using drugs or alcohol. I have to face my fears, confront my resentments, and look in the mirror to say definitively: *"I'm proud of you. You are worthy. And most importantly, I love you."*

That level of curing doesn't happen by accident. It takes consistent sobriety, yes—but it also requires time alone, doing the honest, soul-searching work necessary to process and heal.

I talk to a lot of people who tell me, *"I haven't had a drink in a year, two years, even three years, but I'm still not happy."* They assume that sobriety alone should fix everything, that life should magically feel good just because they're not drinking or using anymore.

But here's the truth: *the absence of drugs and alcohol doesn't make you happy.*

Being happy comes from facing your past. It comes from processing the pain, the injuries, the abuse—whatever it was that you've been running from. Whether it's trauma inflicted by a parent, a teacher, an abuser, or anyone else, those experiences don't just disappear when you put down the drink or the drug.

Recovery is about turning toward those things instead of running from them. It's about facing them head-on, acknowledging the pain, and doing the work to heal.

I'm not saying this is easy; far from it. But I've learned that true remedial starts when you stop suppressing those feelings with substances and start addressing them. Therapy, reflection, and consistent work on yourself are necessary steps. Because recovery isn't just about not drinking; it's about creating a life you can be proud of. It's about being okay with yourself, with the way people treat you, and with the way you treat others.

Sobriety is the first step, but recovery is the journey of healing your mind, body, and spirit. And the only way to truly recover is to face the pain, process it, and let it go.

***

The feelings don't just go away when you stop drinking or using drugs. They'll still show up— anger, frustration, abandonment, loneliness. And when they do, the key is learning how to sit with those feelings without reaching for a substance to numb them.

Everyone uses substances to run from something. The real work begins when you ask yourself: *What am I running from?*

When I know the source of the pain, I can confront it. I can heal it. It's like going to the doctor with an injury. If I say my elbow hurts and the doctor's solution is to amputate my arm, that's extreme. There are better ways to treat the problem, but I can't address it if I don't know what's wrong.

For years, if I felt treated unfairly in business or by my family, I'd drown those emotions in alcohol or drugs. It didn't matter if it was anger, sadness, or disappointment—there was always a drink or a pill to take the edge off. But the more I relied on substances to escape, the more I lost my ability to face life.

Even in sobriety, those feelings still arise. People still treat me unfairly. Life still throws curveballs. But the difference is today, I don't let those emotions dictate my actions. I've learned to acknowledge them, sit with them, and address them.

For example, anger used to be my automatic response. Someone would yell, and I'd yell back, break something, or storm off. Then, I'd feel bad about it and drink the guilt away. But now, when anger rises, I pause. I don't give in. Over time, I've retrained myself. I'm not as reactive as I once was, and I don't need substances to calm me down.

Some feelings, though, are harder to identify—like abandonment or loneliness. These are often tied to old wounds and unresolved trauma. The pain may feel the same as it did 15 or 20 years ago because it's triggering something deeper. Until those triggers are addressed, recovery can't happen.

For years, we have come up with extreme measures to protect ourselves—using drugs, alcohol, or other destructive habits to avoid the pain. But once we stop running, we realize we don't need to numb the hurt. We can address it, and with time, we can recover.

***

Even after years of sobriety, feelings still pop up. I'm over four years clean, and I still have moments where I feel anger or frustration. Just the other day, I had to visit a client who was upset about part of a job. In the past, her anger would have triggered mine, and I would've responded with frustration or rage. But not anymore.

Instead, I approached the situation calmly. I didn't match her anger with anger. I didn't go home and drink it away. I handled it. And afterward, I chose joy. I laughed about it. I moved on.

This is what recovery looks like. It's not about suppressing emotions or pretending they don't exist. It's about addressing the feelings and choosing to respond differently.

***

Trauma can keep us stuck if we don't face it. Whether it's a childhood experience, a bad relationship, or an event like September 11th, the hurt doesn't have to define us forever. People who lost loved ones on that tragic day didn't all vow never to fly again or avoid New York City forever. They faced their pain and found ways to move forward.

In the same way, I've learned to stop carrying the weight of old wounds. Those experiences happened, but they don't have to dictate how I live today.

Recovery and healing go hand in hand. They're synonyms. Recovery means I've healed—or at least, I'm actively working towards it. It means letting go of the weight of the past so I can fully live in the present.

That process starts with identifying what hurt me. Maybe it was a childhood wound, like not making the junior varsity baseball team or being treated unfairly by a teacher. Those feelings of rejection or not being "good enough" lingered for years. But when I finally faced them, I realized they didn't have to hold power over me anymore.

Recovery is about recognizing these patterns, addressing them, and learning how to respond to life differently.

Drugs and alcohol don't make me happy. Staying sober doesn't make me happy. Mending, growing, and living a life I'm proud of—that's what makes me happy. And that's what recovery is all about.

Early in sobriety, I wasn't satisfied with just being uncomfortable. I didn't want to live in a constant state of unease. So, I committed to doing the work—facing my past, identifying my triggers, and changing my behaviors.

It's about becoming whole again. And that means addressing every part of your life—your mind, your body, and your spirit.

Chapter 7
Roll Up Your Sleeves

As February began to warm up, so did something inside me. There was an awakening—a sense that life was coming back to me. But even with that flicker of light, I knew something still wasn't right. Physically, I was improving. I looked better, moved better, and even felt better in my body. But mentally, emotionally, spiritually—there was still a weight I couldn't quite name.

That's when I remembered what my friend Sonny had told me about the program of Alcoholics Anonymous. *"You have to take a personal inventory."*

I knew it was time.

One morning, I walked into Grove Coffee, a place I had been to so many times before, but today felt different. There was a heaviness to it, an unspoken gravity pulling me to this table, to this moment.

I sat down, set my notebook in front of me, and took a deep breath.

In the background, the hum of espresso machines filled the air. The scent of freshly brewed coffee wrapped around me, blending with the distant sound of milk being frothed and orders being called out.

Every few minutes, the door would swing open, and a beam of sunlight would stretch across the floor, hitting my table as if to remind me: *This is exactly where you need to be.*

I stared at the blank page in front of me. This wasn't just a list. This was a reckoning.

I pressed my pencil to the paper and began.

Nicole.

Brett.

Mom.

Dorothy.

And then, the weight of the pencil became unbearable. My hand hesitated. My breath caught in my throat.

For the first time, I wrote down a name I had never dared to face.

Dad.

At that moment, in a coffee shop in Chandler, Arizona, a 45-year-old man realized—maybe for the first time in his life—that he had *daddy issues*.

I had been making conscious decisions my whole life based on unconscious hurts—trauma and events that I didn't even fully remember until that moment. Sitting in that coffee shop, staring at the names on my list, I saw the patterns for the first time.

At six months old, I had been left at my grandparents' house, abandoned by my parents. And for the rest of my life—whether I realized it or not— I had been performing for an audience that wasn't even watching. Every action, every achievement, every moment of striving to be *enough* had been driven by a single, unspoken hope: that my dad would come back and pick me up.

The voices in my head echoed that same rejection. The same voices I had heard earlier in my journey—the ones from my so-called friends saying, *we don't want him here. Don't bring him to my house. He can't be around my family.* That night had felt like an isolated incident, but now I understood— it was just another version of the same story I had been telling myself since childhood.

***

For most of my life, I didn't recognize this for what it was. Instead, I performed. Unconsciously, I worked to prove I was worthy.

As a kid, I needed to win. If there was a game, a contest, or a competition, I had to come out on top. I chased trophies—whatever they looked like in life—because winning meant people would see me, acknowledge me, and validate me. *You're a winner. You're good. You're amazing.*

And maybe, just maybe, someone would say, *you remind me of your father.* But in my mind, that wasn't a compliment. That was the reason he didn't want me.

Without even realizing it, I had carried that resentment into adulthood. I wasn't walking around thinking, *Oh, I'm an abandoned kid,* but that belief was ingrained in me. The snippets of life—the comments, the labels, the dismissals—became the foundation for how I saw myself.

You'll never amount to anything. You'll never succeed. Those words may have been spoken decades ago, but I had spent my entire life trying to prove them wrong.

So now, I ask the reader: Who are you still reacting to? Who are you deflecting, dismissing, or fighting with because of something that was said to you years ago? Are you giving attitude to your spouse because of something a teacher told you in high school? Are you overreacting to a coworker because of something a friend said in college?

We all do this. We all carry old wounds into new situations. And unless we recognize it, those wounds shape our reactions.

That's where *compound trauma* comes in. Compound trauma is a cycle—an accumulation of pain that builds over time, making us react to *this* moment based on *that* moment years ago.

Picture this: A teacher once told me, *You're not good enough.* Twenty-two years later, my wife says something completely innocent, but my brain twists it. *She's going to leave you.* Now, I'm reacting to her with the same fear of abandonment I've carried since childhood.

She wasn't leaving. She wasn't even thinking about leaving. But I *heard* it in her words.

It's the same with my daughters. Sometimes, they'll say something that reminds me of my high school classmates who were cruel to me. And suddenly, I'm not responding to my daughters—I'm responding to those scars from decades ago.

It happens in an instant. A single sentence. A single look. And before I know it, my night is ruined. My week is ruined. My relationships suffer. And yet, the person I'm reacting to isn't actually the one who hurt me.

***

Sitting in that coffee shop, I remembered something Maria had once said in a meeting: *"My soul is on a budget. I can no longer afford fear, anger, and resentment."*

I couldn't afford it either. I had been carrying anger toward my father for years. But what I hadn't realized was that I had projected that anger onto my brother, too. Why? Because I had convinced myself that my dad *chose* him instead of me.

But when I looked at the situation honestly, I saw the truth: My father was 19 years old when he had me. He was just a kid himself. His own father had abandoned him when he was ten. And like so many others before him, he simply did what had been done to him. That didn't excuse his choices, but it allowed me to give him grace.

***

Healing felt like unpacking a heavy backpack—one I had been carrying for so long that I didn't even realize the weight of it. One by one, I started pulling out the stones.

I wrote down names. Situations. Conversations. I let myself feel every emotion I had been avoiding. Minutes turned into hours as I sat there, filling page after page.

With every word I wrote, the weight began to lift.

***

Steve-O once described recovery in three words:

Uncover, discover, discard.

Uncover what hurt me.

Discover where it came from.

Discard the weight I no longer need to carry.

By uncovering the truth about my father, I could finally see the full picture. By discovering his story—his own pain, his own trauma—I could give him grace. And by discarding the anger and resentment I had carried for so long, I could finally lighten my load.

I had spent years holding resentment toward my wife simply because *she didn't have to face the things I did.* She never knew abandonment, sexual abuse, divorce, or financial struggle. And in my addiction, that became my safety net—*You don't know what it's like to be me.*

But that mindset kept me stuck. It made her the enemy when she wasn't.

And so I say to the reader: *The person in front of you isn't the one hurting you.*

There's no point in coiling up and striking back at the people in your life today over wounds from your past. It does no good to hold resentment against family members who don't even know they've hurt you.

The moment I began to release those burdens, I started to free myself from the bondage of my past. This was where I learned to respond instead of react. This was where I stopped hearing my wife's words, as if they were spoken by a high school bully. This was where I stopped taking my daughters' questions as an attack.

This was where I finally understood that *healing is possible.*

But first, I had to roll up my sleeves and do the work.

***

There are so many times in life when our day is determined by the way we interact with people.

For years, I reacted to everything—big or small—with the same intensity. If someone cut me off in traffic, I took it personally. If someone spoke to me in a sharp tone, I felt attacked. My default setting was anger, and I carried it like a weapon, ready to fire at any moment.

But today, I try to respond differently.

There was one morning early in recovery when I was driving on an Arizona freeway, just like any other day. I noticed a car behind me, weaving in and out of lanes, headlights bouncing as it darted between vehicles. He was driving recklessly—cutting people off, pushing his way forward.

I felt my blood pressure rise.

97

He eventually passed me, speeding ahead, still weaving dangerously through traffic. A few miles down the road, I pulled off to get gas, and there he was—at a pump.

My anger flared. This is my chance to let him have it.

I walked toward him, my mind already constructing the words. Nice driving, jerk. In a bit of a hurry, huh?

But before I could unload, he turned to me, his face etched with panic.

"Yeah," he said. "My daughter was just in a car accident. I'm trying to get to her."

And just like that, my anger evaporated.

I had been so ready to judge him, to assume the worst, to make his driving about me. But in reality, he was just a father racing to be with his child—doing exactly what I would have done if I were in his shoes.

That moment shifted something in me.

I started to realize that the emotions that rise up in the morning—frustration, anger, stress—are often just a reflection of something deeper. The guy who snapped at me for being three minutes late wasn't really mad about my tardiness. The coworker who sent an aggressive email wasn't truly upset about a missing attachment. They were reacting to something else—maybe an argument with their spouse, a health scare, financial stress, or a family emergency.

And I had a choice.

I could match their energy, escalate the tension, and let anger dictate my day.

Or, I could be the person who breaks the cycle.

Today, when someone lashes out at me, I try to say, "I don't know what you're going through, but I'm sorry."

Not sorry in a way that admits fault, but sorry in a way that extends grace.

Because I know they're not truly upset with me. They're carrying burdens I can't see. And the moment I become a source of love, kindness, and light—just like the Eleventh Step Prayer teaches—the dynamic shifts.

Anger dissolves. Fear weakens. Resentment fades.

Not just for me but for them too.

I've realized that by responding with patience instead of aggression, I make my life more manageable. And in doing so, I make their life a little easier, too.

A single kind response can diffuse a situation that otherwise would have spiraled into conflict. A moment of compassion can take someone from feeling unseen and unheard to feel acknowledged and understood.

But I wouldn't have learned any of this if I hadn't first recognized my own patterns—if I hadn't uncovered my own anger, discovered where it came from, and discarded the weight of it.

I visualize it like carrying a backpack—one that's been weighing me down for years.

Every grudge, every wound, every past hurt is a stone I've packed inside. I've carried this heavy load everywhere, feeling the weight of it but never stopping to unpack it.

But now, I'm unzipping the bag. One by one, I'm taking out the burdens I no longer need.

I used to think that anger and resentment protected me, that they made me strong. But now I see that strength comes in letting go. I realized that most of what I carried wasn't mine, to begin with.

So today, I keep my soul on a budget.

I can't afford anger.

I can't afford resentment.

I can't afford fear.

Because the cost of carrying those things is too high.

Instead, I choose peace. I choose grace. I choose to roll up my sleeves, do the work, and lighten the load—one stone at a time.

I want to spend some time talking about that backpack. Not just mine, but yours. Because we all carry one.

For years, I had been lugging around a heavy, invisible weight—stuffed full of sadness, trauma, fear, rejection, and resentment. I had been carrying stones that weren't even mine, to begin with. And like so many others, I picked up drugs, alcohol, food, pornography, gambling—anything I could—to avoid feeling what those stones actually weighed.

These addictions became a distraction. A numbing agent. A way to convince myself the weight wasn't really there.

But here's the truth: The weight doesn't just disappear because you ignore it. The pain doesn't go away just because you try to drown it in alcohol or bury it under a pile of distractions. It's still there, dragging behind you, making everything in life feel just a little bit harder.

That morning at Grove Coffee, as I sat with my notebook, I finally unzipped my backpack.

I started pulling out the stones, one by one.

The things people had said.

The people who had let me down.

The moments that made me feel abandoned, unworthy, or unloved.

Each name I wrote, each resentment I faced, was like placing another heavy rock on the table in front of me. And I realized something—I had been carrying this weight my whole life, but I never once stopped to ask if I needed to carry it.

Now, I want the reader to picture their own backpack.

Imagine sitting down right now and unzipping it.

What's inside?

Maybe it's the way your father spoke to you when you were young.

Maybe it's the way your mother made you feel like you weren't enough.

Maybe it's something a teacher said in passing, but it stuck.

Maybe it's the betrayal of a friend.

Maybe it's the pain of a relationship that ended without closure.

Whatever it is—whatever has been living inside that backpack for years—it's time to take it out. Lay it all on the table. Name it. Write it down. Because if you don't, it will continue to own space in your mind and weigh you down in ways you don't even realize.

And here's the thing: When I picked up that stone of abandonment, I didn't just carry it—I acted on it. I performed, hoping to be seen. I built walls, expecting rejection. I avoided intimacy because, deep down, I believed people would leave me.

We do this with all our wounds.

We carry resentment, and suddenly, every new relationship feels unsafe.

We carry fear, and suddenly, every opportunity feels like a risk.

We carry rejection, and suddenly, we sabotage good things before they even have a chance to take root.

This is what compound trauma does—it keeps us trapped in old pain, reacting to new moments based on past wounds.

What are you still carrying that no longer serves you? What words, what memories, what painful experiences are still weighing down your steps, even when you think you've moved on?

I don't just want you to take the stones out and look at them. I want you to get rid of them.

That thing your teacher said? Toss it. It has no power over you anymore.

That moment of rejection? It's done. It can't touch who you are today.

That betrayal? Let it go. You don't need to carry the weight of someone else's choices.

Throw the stones in the river. Drop them by the side of the road. Do whatever you need to do, but don't keep stuffing them back in your backpack.

This is how we get free.

This is how we recover.

***

I sat in that coffee shop for over six hours, writing, remembering, and unpacking.

At one point, I walked outside just to breathe, and new memories surfaced. More stones to lay down.

And in that moment, I felt something I hadn't felt in years: *light.*

Not just physically but emotionally. Mentally. Spiritually.

For the first time, I didn't feel weighed down by my past.

And the beauty of it all? I realized that this isn't a one-time thing. This is a practice. A daily decision.

Every day, I get the chance to unpack what I don't need. Every day, I get to choose which stones I carry and which ones I leave behind.

And every day, my life becomes just a little lighter.

***

Unpacking my past was one thing. But now, I had to learn how to unpack *today.*

The guy at the grocery store is taking too long.

The kids are testing my patience.

My finances are stressing me out.

If I'm not careful, I start repacking my backpack all over again, carrying today's frustrations into tomorrow. And when I do that enough times, it piles up. The weight grows. Before I know it, I'm back to dragging around burdens I don't even need to carry.

That's the difference between *now* and five years ago.

Back then, I had no idea I was even carrying anything. I was just reacting—blindly, emotionally, destructively—to a life that felt heavy without understanding why. I didn't know that I had the ability to *choose* which burdens I carried. I didn't know that I could *unpack* my past and set it down for good.

And the best part of this six-hour, painstaking self-discovery? *Nobody else had to tell me what was wrong with me.* I wasn't sitting in a therapy session, waiting for someone to diagnose my wounds. I wasn't listening to someone else tell me why I was broken. I *decided for myself* what I wanted to face. I uncovered my own pain. I named my own fears. I held each one in my hands and made the choice—*Do I still want to carry this?*

***

Now, understand that you don't have to sit in a coffee shop for six hours to do this. You don't have to write until your hand cramps, your heartaches, and your eyes blur with tears.

But you *do* have to start unpacking. I want to make something clear—unpacking isn't easy. There are stones in that backpack that won't just disappear because you recognize them. Some wounds require therapy, deep work, and patience. And there are some wounds that won't be healed overnight. Some scars need more than just recognition—they need *time*. But don't believe the old adage that *"time heals all wounds."* It doesn't.

Time doesn't heal anything. Time only makes wounds more forgettable. And if you're not careful, time will trick you into thinking you're fine when, really, you're still carrying the same weight you've had for decades.

That was me. Forty-some years had passed, and I was still walking around as a wounded baby—completely unaware. But because of this painstaking effort, because of this self-discovery, I finally have a choice.

And here's the most beautiful part of it all: Now that I've torn everything down, I *get to rebuild.*

I get to start fresh with a foundation built on truth. I get to design a life that isn't shaped by old wounds. I get to carry forward only what serves me.

And now, *so do you.*

So, as you sit with your own backpack, as you sift through your own burdens, ask yourself: What do I need to heal from? What am I still carrying that I don't have to?

Because from this moment on, you are no longer required to carry the weight of the past. You get to rebuild.

***

We all carry a backpack.

Maybe yours is packed with abandonment like mine was. Maybe it's loaded with the weight of sexual trauma, something you've never spoken out loud. Maybe it's the sting of emotional abuse, the scars of a toxic relationship. Maybe you were the kid who was always told you weren't smart enough, fast enough, pretty enough. Maybe someone made you believe you were unlovable.

Whatever it is, I want you to picture it—your own backpack.

For years, you've been hauling it around, some days heavier than others, but always there. You've tried to ignore it. You've convinced yourself it doesn't really affect you. But it does.

It shapes how you see yourself.

It determines what you believe you deserve.

It dictates how you react to the world around you.

And the worst part? You might not even realize it.

I didn't.

I thought I was just an angry guy, a guy who liked to party, a guy who had a short temper and a reckless streak. I thought my actions were just who I was.

But the truth? I was reacting. I was reacting to a father who never came back for me. I was reacting to voices from my past that told me I wasn't good enough. I was reacting to wounds I had never stopped to heal.

And so I drank. I used. I numbed. Because I thought if I didn't feel it, it wouldn't be real.

But in that coffee shop, with the sun spilling through the door and my hand aching from writing, I realized—this weight had been mine to carry, but it was also mine to set down.

So now, I ask you: What are you carrying? What words, what wounds, what memories are still living in your backpack? What have you packed away so deep that you've convinced yourself it doesn't matter anymore—when, really, it still controls you?

Your life is *not* the sum of every bad thing that's ever been said about you.

If enough people told you that you weren't good enough, maybe you started to believe it. If someone made you feel like you deserved abuse, maybe you stayed longer than you should have. If the world convinced you that you were worthless, maybe you settled for a life that's less than you deserve.

But that is not who you are. You are not just a collection of past pain. You are not bound by what has happened to you. You are not required to carry this weight forever.

Unpack because once you do, you'll realize what I did: *There is a mountain of pain that you no longer have to carry.* You get to choose what stays and what goes. You get to pick what you take with you into tomorrow.

This is the point where you get to decide. Are you going to keep carrying what was never yours to hold? Or are you finally going to set it down?

Are you going to let the words and wounds of others dictate your future? Or are you going to build something new? Because that's what comes next.

Once you've done the work—once you've rolled up your sleeves and faced what's been hiding in the depths of your life—then, and only then, do you get to start rebuilding.

Chapter 8
The Remodel

Some weeks had passed since taking a full inventory of my life. Once I had stripped away all the fake facades—the distractions, the self-imposed expectations, the toxic relationships, and the numbing agents—I was left with an empty shell.

It was almost like a bus driver departing with no people on board. Imagine getting on an empty bus and slipping into the seat. For the first time, however, I was the driver and not just a passenger. Nevertheless, nobody else was on board. For so long, I had allowed whoever or whatever wanted to hop on—people, emotions, habits—without giving it a second thought. I let fear and anger sit in the front row. I let chaos buckle itself in without question. I never considered who deserved a seat on my journey or if they were driving me somewhere, I actually wanted to go.

Now, that choice was mine. I was in charge of who boarded, who remained, and who I would let off at the next stop for the first time. It was an exciting and terrifying realization. If I was truly in charge of this bus—my life—what stops would I skip? Who would I allow to join me? And most importantly, what kind of life was I willing to build?

***

Learning to forgive both myself and other people was one of the most crucial phases in this rebuilding process. It seemed like I had unwittingly let people on my bus—resentment, remorse, and old grief. They kept me mired in old habits, distracted me, and depleted me. I understood that I had to create space for healing if I wanted to carry on.

It was difficult to forgive. I initially believed it meant forgiving the acts of people who had harmed me. However, I discovered that genuine forgiveness was about releasing myself from the burden of holding onto the past, not about defending it.

I found it most difficult to forgive myself. I had been my own harshest critic for years, clinging to remorse and shame as if they were essential burdens. I had to accept that although I couldn't alter the past, I could influence the future. I was able to embrace change and believe that I was deserving of another shot by letting go of my self-judgment.

***

Then, one seemingly insignificant moment changed the trajectory of my life.

It wasn't a grand occasion, not a major event, not a celebration. It happened in the quiet of my own home. Nearly a year into my sobriety, my daughter Autumn called out from the kitchen.

"Hey, Dad, what are you doing tonight?"

Understand—Autumn and I had never had the smoothest relationship. We were alike in so many ways, which sometimes meant we clashed more than we connected. Even after I had quit drinking and using, there remained an unspoken distance between us. I had hoped that my sobriety alone would bridge the gap, but relationships don't heal simply because one person changes.

Nevertheless, her questioning triggered an inward reaction in me. I answered, "I really don't have any plans." "How about you?"

She paused for a second. "Want to join me at the driving range since Mom is working late?"

Something clicked at once. Golf wasn't the topic. It has nothing to do with the actual activity. She wanted to be with me, that's why. She wanted her dad there, but not because she had to or because she felt sorry for him.

I experienced something I hadn't felt in a while that evening at the driving range. Unadulterated happiness. The kind of happiness that cannot be produced by drugs or approval from others. A father and his daughter were playing golf beneath the floodlights; there were no loud parties, flashing lights, or other distractions. It was simple and significant.

Everything changed in that instant. It changed my perspective on all relationships, not just the one I had with Autumn. I mistook chaos for friendship and volume for connection for a very long time. In actuality, though, the folks who really mattered were able to get a seat on my bus when I had finally gotten rid of the commotion.

***

I wanted to sit next to Autumn instead of her being a faraway traveler in my life. Others brought serenity, love, and contentment with them as they boarded. As I packed my bus with these individuals, I came to the realization that I might live a fulfilling life free from fear, greed, and the never-ending quest for approval from others.

As I went along, I started to be more deliberate about who I let along the way. My wife, my daughters, and the people who really inspired me were among the passengers who were given preference seating. I sat others in the back row until I was sure they were worthy of a closer seat. At the following stop, I knew I had to let go of those. No matter how familiar they were, some relationships, feelings, and habits no longer had a place in my life.

I began to assess my life more clearly. I stopped at spots that made me feel exhausted. I stopped going to addresses that made me feel my worst. Bars, casinos, poisonous settings, and even fast-food drive-thrus that numbed me in their own way are just a few of the places that the old me would have allowed my bus to roll into. However, I now understood that I was not required to travel someplace I did not choose to. I didn't have to stop at worthless addresses.

And I started to be picky about my habits, just like I was picky about my passengers. I looked for pursuits that enhanced my life, such as yoga, golf, hiking, and music. Things that brought me calm instead of taking it away. Every new habit brought with it new people, and accountability accompanied those new people. And one of the most effective strategies I discovered for rebuilding was accountability.

Someone who simply goes with you when things are easy is not a loyal friend. Someone who warns you not to stop at the spots that have previously misled you is a true friend. "We don't need to go there anymore," they are the ones stating. They assist you in seeing that joy is not concealed in excess, and that enjoyment need not be found in devastation.

Thus, the remodeling proceeded. I reviewed my belongings on my bus every day. On certain days, I discovered baggage—doubt, self-criticism, and resentment—left by an old traveler. However, I had the ability to open the doors, let go of that baggage, and continue on.

The goal of this travel was not to arrive at a destination. It wasn't about being flawless. It involved making deliberate decisions each day regarding my possessions, the people I chose to surround myself with, and the things I aimed to create.

I realized something as I glanced in my rearview mirror: the road ahead was full of possibilities, while the road behind me was getting narrower.

It was the first time I wasn't just getting by.

I was behind the wheel.

Chapter 9
Thank you For The Heart Attack

After nearly nine months of sobriety, my sponsor encouraged me to take the next step in my recovery journey. The 12th step of Alcoholics Anonymous emphasizes carrying the message to those still suffering. One morning, when the question was posed—"Is anyone willing to be a sponsor?"—I hesitantly raised my hand.

The meeting concluded, and a man named Pete approached me. He asked if I would sit down with him and possibly become his sponsor. I wasn't sure if I was ready for that responsibility. How could I guide someone else when I still felt like I was figuring things out myself? But I agreed to meet him for coffee the following morning, unsure of what this new chapter in my recovery would look like.

The next day, I pulled up to the coffee shop with apprehension pressing against my ribs. Could I really be of help to someone else? Was I qualified to lead anyone through this journey?

When I stepped inside, my eyes darted across the room until they landed on Pete. He sat hunched in a chair, hands wrapped around a cheap gas station coffee, his fingers twitching slightly. Our backgrounds, our demographics, even our drug of choice—everything about us seemed different. But the more we spoke, the more I realized how similar our experiences were.

Pete opened up about his past, about how addiction had taken hold of him at a young age. He told me about a traumatic event when he was just twelve years old. He had been at a lake in Arizona with his brother, and in a moment that would define his life, Pete had watched his brother drown. He had tried to save him, but he couldn't. The weight of that loss became unbearable, and Pete sought an escape with drugs and alcohol. His first experience with heroin came on his high school graduation day, and from that moment forward, he was hooked.

By the time we met, Pete had been using it for over forty years. He had lost everything—his family, his home, his self-worth. At one point, he had been living in a shed adjacent to the home his parents had left him, unable to pay property taxes. When the state finally ordered him to vacate, Pete had hit rock bottom. He had cried out to a God he didn't believe in, pleading for a way to come up with the $5,000 he needed to keep his house.

Within 48 hours, Pete was hit by a delivery truck outside a Walmart in Show Low, Arizona. It wasn't a serious accident, but the insurance company quickly sought to settle. Their first offer? Exactly $5,000.

Pete told me this story with tears in his eyes. "And do you know what I did with that money?" he asked. I assumed he had paid his back taxes and saved his home. Instead, he said, "I bought $5,000 worth of heroin."

Even when given a way out, Pete chose addiction. His pain was too great, and even a miraculous financial lifeline couldn't fix the wounds he carried inside.

But somehow, Pete found his way to sobriety. His sobriety date, February 14th—Valentine's Day—became a bright spot in our friendship. My wife, Nicole, and I made it a tradition to celebrate with him every year. We saw Pete not just as a man in recovery but as someone who had become a part of our family.

Time passed by at its own pace, but then, three months after his third sober anniversary, I got a call. A call that was like a gut punch.

My phone buzzed violently, and a mutual friend's voice—raw, breathless, fraying at the edges—crackled through the speaker: "Pete's having a heart attack. I think he's *dead*."

Time froze. Then adrenaline surged, sharp and metallic. "Call 911 now!" I barked, already sprinting to my car. As I bolted to my car, my hands were shaking. I fumbled with the keys.

The engine roared to life, and I tore out of the driveway, tires screeching against the pavement. Every red light felt like a cruel joke, each second stretching endlessly as I weaved through traffic, willing my car to go faster. By the time I arrived at Pete's house, the ambulance was gone. A single police officer remained with his face grim.

"He flatlined twice," the officer said. "They got him back, but it's bad."

I barely registered the words before I was back in my car, my pulse pounding in my ears as I sped to the hospital. Pete had finally gotten his life back, and now, just as things were turning around, death was looming over him. I knew how much he feared dying. He had told me before that the idea of death terrified him—not because he was afraid of what came after, but because he wasn't ready. He felt there were still things left undone, relationships left unfixed.

The hospital corridor swallowed me— fluorescent lights buzzing, antiseptic stinging my nostrils. Nurses bustled like ghosts in scrubs. When the surgeon emerged, scanning for family, I lunged forward. "I'm his person," I insisted, voice cracking. The truth hung heavy: Pete had no one else. I realized how alone he had been.

They let me see him. The ICU hummed with machines, their rhythmic beeps a macabre soundtrack. Pete lay motionless, skin ashen, tubes snaking from his arms. But when I whispered his name, his eyelids fluttered. A ghost of a smile. "That… was a close one," he rasped, each word a struggle.

I asked if there was anything I could do for him, expecting him to make some final request. Instead, he surprised me. "I want to have a meal with my sister."

That was his dying wish. Not money, not possessions. Just a meal with his estranged sister.

I didn't know if she would be willing to see him. Pete had told me before that she wanted nothing to do with him. But I promised him I would try.

I scoured Facebook, digging through old photos, cross-referencing mutual friends, and clicking through endless profiles. Nothing!

I tried variations of her name and different spellings. Then, finally, a hit—a man with her last name, likely her son. My hands hovered over the keyboard before I typed out a message, explaining who I was and what had happened to Pete. I hit send, heart hammering as I stared at my phone, waiting.

Twelve torturous hours later, my phone erupted—the caller ID read Yuma, Arizona.

"Hello?" I answered cautiously.

A woman's voice came through the speaker. "Is this Tracy?"

It was her. Pete's sister.

"I'm already driving," she said, voice quaking. "I… I didn't think he'd ever…" She trailed off, swallowed by decades of regret. "I never thought my brother would ever want to talk to me again after how I treated him the last time I saw him," she admitted. But now, knowing he had asked for her, she was eager to see him.

When they reunited, the air crackled—awkward hugs, tear-streaked faces, unspoken apologies. But in that sterile room, something fractured began to mend.

Pete and his sister were reunited before his surgery. Their fractured relationship found a moment of healing. And a few days later, when I visited him after his successful quadruple bypass, Pete was smiling. He looked at me and said six words I will never forget: "Thank God for the heart attack."

Pete understood what most of us fail to grasp—sometimes, our biggest struggles are the very things that lead us to healing. His heart attack brought him back to his sister. It gave him another chance.

A recent reel that went viral on social media vividly encapsulates the dilemma we often face when it comes to valuing life. The host of the video posed a simple yet profound question: Would you accept a gift of one million dollars? Naturally, the entire audience eagerly agreed. But then came the caveat. The money would come with the knowledge that tomorrow would be your last day on earth. Instantly, every hand was lowered. The excitement faded, and the room grew quiet. The host then offered his real lesson: if, in fact, you would choose another day over a huge windfall, why do we not treat each day with the same value? This moment was a stark reminder of how fragile life truly is. For Pete, his heart attack served as a cruel wake-up call—life is both fragile and precious, and every moment is worth cherishing.

That moment forced me to ask myself: What am I grateful for? Not just the good things, but the struggles, the setbacks, the slow traffic, the unexpected delays. Do I only practice gratitude when life is going well, or can I be thankful for the challenges that shape me?

As of the writing of this book, Pete is over four and a half years sober. He continues to build his life, to grow, and to strengthen his relationship with his family. His story reminds me that every moment— good or bad—has the potential to add meaning to our lives.

So, I'll leave you with this question: Are we going to be people who divide and subtract, or will we choose to add and multiply?

Chapter 10
Mess To Message

I can still hear the rhythmic click-clack of Miss Humphrey's chalk against the board, her cursive numbers looping like poetry.

Fourth-grade math was my sanctuary: problems had answers, equations balanced, and chaos resolved into order. *Seven times four? Twenty-eight. Every time.* Life felt solvable, a series of neat black-and-white truths. But decades later, I'd learn that sobriety isn't arithmetic—it's algebra. Variables shift. Unknowns linger. And the deepest equations aren't solved with numbers but with the messy, luminous calculus of the heart.

There isn't always a single right answer. There are variables we can't control, equations that never seem to balance, and numbers that don't add up no matter how many times we try to solve for x.

And the most complicated math of all?

The math of *people.*

In math, you know immediately if you've gotten something wrong.

In life, you can pour years of energy into a relationship, a job, or a dream—only to wake up one day and realize the numbers never worked in the first place.

I spent years measuring my success by business profits, bank account balances, and material possessions. But when I took a hard look at my relationships, my energy, and what I was actually building—things didn't add up.

I had surrounded myself with people who were subtracting and dividing.

People who drained my energy instead of adding to it.

People who multiplied my problems instead of my joy.

And when I finally got sober, I realized that the equation of my life needed serious adjustment.

Sobriety is not the goal. Sobriety is the *gift*.

It's the gift that allows me to rewrite the formula. To determine what I want to *add* to my life and what I refuse to let *subtract* from it anymore.

You've seen the movies. Addiction is a dimly lit montage of empty bottles, trembling hands, and rain-streaked windows. The soundtrack swells with despair. It's obvious, almost cartoonish—look how far they've fallen.

But real addiction isn't a screenplay. It's quieter. It's waking up in a life that feels like someone else's, where the darkness isn't the absence of light but the absence of love. You don't notice the fog until you're choking on it.

Sobriety, though, isn't the credits rolling. It's the projector flipping on, illuminating the equations you've ignored:

The Real Equation

At the end of Chapter 9, I asked: Are you adding and multiplying, or subtracting and dividing?

Sobriety isn't the solution—it's the gift of a clean whiteboard. Now you get to solve for X, where X is the life you're rebuilding. Here's my formula:

1. Protection (Safety = Boundaries)

Every human craves safety. Not just physical but emotional—guarding your time, energy, and peace.

In addiction, I let chaos colonize me. Now? I subtract what harms and add what heals.

2.   Support (Teamwork > Isolation)

Sobriety isn't a solo mission. You need allies—people who don't just cheer but fight for you. Subtract the critics; multiply the ones who see your light even when you're dim.

3.   Guidance (Wisdom = Borrowed Eyes)

I used to think asking for help was a weakness. Now I know: mentors are living equations. They've solved for pain; let their answers guide your variables.

4.   Motivation (Urgency ≠ Desperation)

Addiction is desperate. Recovery is urgent—a fire to live, not just survive. Subtract complacency; add purpose.

5.   Fulfillment (Joy = Inner Algebra)

Happiness? Fleeting. Fulfillment is solving for the constants: gratitude, service, and stillness. It's the sum of small moments.

6. Teaching (Growth = Shared Lessons)

Your mess isn't a failure—it's a curriculum. Subtract shame; multiply your story. Someone's waiting to learn from your equation.

From problem to proof – in math, proofs validate truth. In recovery, your life becomes the proof. The late nights, the hard conversations, the relapses, and restarts—they're not failures. They're steps in the work.

Here is some homework for the heart. Ask:

- *Who or what have I subtracted lately?*
- *What equation am I solving for?*
- *If my life were a movie, what message would the credits roll on?*

Sobriety isn't the answer. It's the sharpened pencil, the blank page. Start writing your proof.

***

Hollywood's addicts are tragic heroes. But you? You're the quiet revolution. The parent who breaks the cycle. The friend who stays. The light refused to be swallowed by the dark.

On a screen, it's easy to see addiction for what it is—dark, desperate, isolating.

But when you're in the middle of it?

You don't see it. You don't recognize the dimness of your own life. You just exist.

***

This chapter is about intentionality.

It's about deciding what we want our lives to be filled with and making sure our equation balances.

Because I can tell you from experience—when your life is full of subtraction and division, the result is always less.

But when you start adding, multiplying, and building something meaningful?

That's where life starts to make sense.

That's where we go from numbers on a page to something deeper.

That's when we take everything we've been through—every miscalculation, every false answer—and turn it into wisdom.

And that's when we realize that life, unlike math, isn't about solving for x.

It's about writing a whole new equation.

***

Think back to when you were a kid.

Remember getting a bad grade on a test? The moment you saw that C- or F, your stomach dropped. You knew you had screwed up.

But then came the best part: the fresh start.

A new semester.

A clean report card.

A chance to do things differently.

Recovery is that fresh start.

But this isn't just about drugs and alcohol. It's about resetting *everything*.

For years, addiction shaped who you spent time with, what you prioritized, and how you viewed yourself.

Now?

You get to rewrite all of it.

You get to decide who belongs in your life.

You get to rebuild healthy habits.

You get to show up in a way that your old self never could.

But sobriety isn't just erasing the red ink. It's handing you a blank sheet. You get to assign the subjects now.

Here's the secret: **recovery isn't subtraction** (stopping the drink, the drug, the chaos). **It's an addition**. You're not just sober—you're rebuilding the curriculum.

There's a moment in early recovery where you realize something:

You're not just quitting something.

You're starting something.

For years, my identity had been tied to the chaos—drinking, using, chasing the next rush. That was the equation I lived by:

More substances = Less reality.

***

The Behaviors We Abandoned (and How to Reclaim Them)

When addiction enrolls you, it starts dropping classes:

- **Physical Education:** The gym bag collects dust. Walks become shuffles. You forget how it feels to crave sweat instead of substances.
- **Social Studies:** Friends who laugh with you get replaced by ones who disappear after you. You stop asking, "How are you?" because you're afraid they'll ask back.
- **Art & Music:** The guitar case stays shut. The sketchbook warps under spilled drinks. Creativity becomes a relic of "the old you."
- **Ethics & Integrity:** Promises dissolve. You stop apologizing because "sorry" feels as empty as your bank account.

But here's the reset: Every day sober is a transfer to a new school. Enrollment is free. The syllabus? Whatever you dare to add.

Your New Curriculum (Swipe Right on These Behaviors)

1. **"Boundaries 101"**
   Old behavior: Saying "yes" to everyone's demands while screaming "no" inside.
   New equation: **Protection = Saying "I'll get back to you" + a 24-hour rule**.
   Vivid shift: Picture your energy as a jar of marble. Every "yes" you don't mean steals a marble. Sobriety teaches you to guard the jar.

2. **"Advanced Vulnerability"**
   Old behavior: Numbing loneliness with substances.
   New equation: **Connection = 1 awkward text + 1 walk with a friend who doesn't need small talk**.
   Vivid shift: Think of the last time you laughed so hard your ribs hurt. That's the sound of subtraction—*one less secret, one less mask*.

3. **"The Joy Elective"**
   Old behavior: Chasing euphoria through a bottle or a bag.
   New equation: **Fulfillment = 10 minutes of morning sun + 1 old hobby resurrected (even badly)**.
   Vivid shift: Remember the first time you

rode a bike? The wobbling, the scraped knees—*and the wind in your face*. Joy isn't perfection. It's showing up.

4. **"Economics of Energy"**
Old behavior: Spending your best hours recovering from hangovers.
New equation: **Investment = 1 hour of sleep > 1 hour of Netflix.**
Vivid shift: Your energy is currency. Sobriety turns you into a millionaire—*stop donating it to dead-end streets.*

The Compounding Interest of Small Changes

Addiction's lie? That "big" moments matter most. But recovery is a math of micro-choices:

- **Day 1:** You drink water instead of vodka.
- **Day 30:** You walk into a coffee shop and recognize your barista's name.
- **Day 100:** You say, "I need help" out loud.
- **Day 365:** Someone says, "You seem... lighter," and you realize they're right.

These aren't just sober days. They're deposits into a life where you're no longer the problem—you're the equation.

***

Here's more homework – homework for the **Reset.**

Grab a pen. Write your new report card. Grade yourself on:

- **Boundaries:** Did I protect my peace?
- **Joy:** Did I create one unapologetically happy moment?
- **Legacy:** Did I add value to someone's life today?

If you flunk? Good. Tomorrow's a fresh page.

Remember: Sobriety isn't your final grade. It's the pencil in your hand.

***

The sneaky part about addiction—it convinces you that this is normal. That living in this gray fog is just the way life is. You don't realize you've been living without color until you step into the light.

And once you do—once you clear the fog and start to rebuild—you have a choice.

You can let your past be nothing more than a pile of broken pieces.

Or you can take those same pieces and turn them into something meaningful.

This is where your mess becomes your message.

This is where your pain turns into purpose.

Because someone out there needs you to show them what's possible.

The darkness they're living in? They don't see it yet.

The lies they're telling themselves? They don't question them yet.

The weight they're carrying? They don't know if they can put it down yet.

But you do.

One day, you'll be the person to expose someone to the love they deserve.

One day, you'll be the reason someone believes change is possible.

I know this because someone did it for me.

And now, it's my responsibility to do it for someone else.

Chapter 11
Love & Light

The dinner table held its usual Wednesday night rhythm—clinking silverware, soft laughter, and the warm glow of the overhead light. But the air hung thick as if the room itself held its breath.

Beneath the surface, a heaviness lingered. A weight pressed down on us, an unspoken tension that tightened our chests. We knew the call was coming. We just didn't know when.

Then, it did. The screen of my phone lit up, cutting through the dimly lit room like a blade. The message was short, but it landed like a gut punch:

If you want to say goodbye, you better come tonight.

The words stole the air from my lungs. I looked at Nicole, my wife, and her face was pale. Within minutes, we rose from the table. Seconds later, we were in the car, speeding toward the hospital, racing against time to say goodbye to one of the greatest gifts I had ever received: my friend, my brother, Sonny.

The highway stretched before us like a grim corridor. The 30-minute drive blurred—streetlights smeared into streaks. The world outside felt muted and distant, like a dream I wasn't quite awake for.

Nicole held my hand, but neither of us spoke. What was there to say? We both knew the reality that awaited us at the end of that highway. We just weren't ready to face it.

When we arrived at the hospital, the stark brightness of the hallways only made the room we entered feel darker. It was small, suffocating, void of any warmth. The hospital room was a tomb of cold fluorescence and mechanical sighs. The beeping of machines provided the only sound, their screens flickering with numbers that meant nothing and everything. A slow, rhythmic reminder that Sonny was still here—but just barely.

Sonny lay motionless, and Michelle, his wife, stood beside him. Her face was carved with exhaustion, grief, and a quiet kind of strength. Her eyes met ours, and they were raw, red-rimmed, and spoke to us. Without words, we understood. *This was it*. This was the last time we'd see them together— Sonny and Michelle, husband and wife, side by side.

Oftentimes, people wear the mask of "everything is fine," but Sonny and Michelle never did. Their truth was raw, transparent. They didn't hide their struggles or pain. They let people in, even when it hurt. And that night, standing in that sterile, lifeless room, the truth was all that remained. Even in this stark finality, there was no pretense. No whispered platitudes. Just the quiet agony of a love facing its last breath.

Nicole gripped my arm, her nails digging into my skin as if anchoring herself to the moment. We stayed as long as we could. Long enough to say everything and nothing at the same time. We stayed until the nurses gently urged us to leave, their voices soft as ghosts.

When we left, we knew we wouldn't be back. We didn't need another visit to confirm what we already knew: Sonny was leaving us.

In the parking lot, Nicole collapsed against me, tears soaking my shirt. "If it weren't for him," she choked, "we wouldn't be here. *We wouldn't be us.*"

The weight of her words sank into me like an anchor. At that moment, I didn't fully grasp their depth. But over the next few days, as grief settled in, I started to understand.

Later that night, my phone lit up again.

He's gone.

After his memorial service, I found myself scrolling through our last conversations. The texts were simple, just the back-and-forth of two friends checking in. But then, buried in the thread, was a link. A YouTube video of a man Sonny often quoted—Wayne Dyer.

I clicked play, and the words struck me like lightning. It was a paraphrase of the 38th verse of Lao Tzu's Tao Te Ching:

The highest good is not to seek to do good but to allow yourself to become it.

That was Sonny. That was the life he lived. He wasn't just a man who did good; he became it. He didn't wear his past as a burden—he used it as fuel to bring love and light into the world.

Memories surged—Sonny's off-key humming, the way he'd slide into a diner booth and order black coffee like it was a sacrament. He'd never preached or proselytized. He'd just been—a flawed, messy beacon who'd shown up, time after time, when I'd given him every reason not to.

Nicole's revelation unfurled slowly. Years earlier, during one of their coffees, Sonny had dismantled her walls with questions she'd never dared to ask herself*: What are you afraid to lose? What's worth fighting for?* She'd left that diner booth with a clarity that saved us—a clarity he'd handed her, no strings attached.

In the days and weeks following his passing, stories of Sonny flooded in. Friends, family, and even distant acquaintances shared how he had touched their lives. His quirks, his struggles, his rough edges—all of it made him who he was. He had seen darkness, lived in it, fought through it. And because of that, he knew how to bring light to others.

For me, that light had come in the form of a well-timed text, an impromptu coffee, a moment of undivided attention. Sonny was never too busy, never too distracted. When he was with you, he was with you. Fully present, fully engaged.

Not all superheroes wear capes. Some wear Pearl Jam T-shirts. Some leave behind fingerprints instead of footprints. Sonny didn't offer me three wishes. He didn't promise me riches or an easy road. He gave me something infinitely more valuable. He gave me another chance.

And for that, he will never be forgotten.

***

I glared at the pamphlet that was given on the day of his celebration of life. The two dates sat there like anchors: January 29, 1973 – January 29, 2025. My tears started dripping onto my jeans until it resembled an untimely accident with an over-filled coffee. I recognized the importance of his dash.

It was a bridge. A testament to the truth that the most fractured stories can mend and that the darkest night can birth the brightest light.

At that moment and because of Sonny Rock's friendship, I remembered that love is not something that you earn; it has to be something you become.

Chapter 12
The Beginning

There's a word "beginning." It means to start… a fresh launch, a new origination? Yes, no, maybe! The meaning of this word shifts depending on where you place the emphasis. You define it according to yourself.

"Ugh… I've got to start all over."

"Yay! Another chance."

Is it a beginning—a fragile, tentative step forward? Or a beginning—a bold declaration of reinvention? For those in recovery, the concept of starting anew is both a gift and a challenge. It carries the weight of past failures and the lightness of untapped potential.

One inspires hope; the other, exhaustion. One is a blank whiteboard, wiped clean and ready for new ideas. The other is the endless struggle of pushing a heavy stone up a mountain over and over again. Perspective determines which version we live in.

Two contrasting images: 1. The Stone. You push a boulder uphill, sweat dripping, muscles burning. It rolls back, and you start again. This is the cycle of addiction—exhausting, repetitive, and defined by struggle. 2. The Whiteboard. Freshly erased, pristine, waiting for new marks. This is recovery: a blank slate, a chance to rewrite your story.

Neither image cancels the other. The stone reminds you of where you've been; the whiteboard invites you to where you're going. My own story unfolded in the tension between these two. I couldn't undo the past but could choose how to frame the future.

I had the power to rewrite my story's ending. The actions I took today, tomorrow, and the day after would shape what came next. This is the pivotal moment when we begin to redefine our purpose.

Change—real, lasting change—starts with us. This isn't self-help fluff—it's physics. It begins with shifting our attention. Practical action paired with ruthless focus creates momentum. But distraction is addiction's favorite trick. I learned this lesson the hard way.

I remember the night my wife whispered to me before I left the house, "Could you please show up at the school tonight sober?" My response? "How sober do you expect me to be? What time is the event?" She sighed, "I really want you to be fully sober because you're leading the halftime show at the girls' basketball game."

I agreed—reluctantly. That morning, I set out with the intention of staying sober, simply to fulfill her request. But intentions without focus are easily derailed. Hours later, I found myself in front of Scratch, a bar I had no business being at. I went inside. One shot turned into three. Three turned into five. Maybe some drugs, too. And then, with blurry confidence, I went off to lead that halftime show.

Disappointment filled her eyes that night. I was the one to blame. Not simply because I drank but because I allowed distraction to override intention. It wasn't the alcohol that failed her—it was my fractured attention. I'd aimed at sobriety but let my focus drift to the siren song of escape. My attention was scattered, and my priorities were misaligned.

Recovery demands more than quitting a substance; it requires redirecting your gaze. Want a bigger house? Okay—but what's the cost if earning it means missing dance recitals and family dinners? For addicts, misplaced attention isn't just unproductive—it's dangerous. Attention is everything. Where we direct our focus determines the course of our lives.

Critics might sneer, and some people will criticize the title of this book—Addict No More. "Once an addict, always an addict," they'll say. To them, I ask: Are you an athlete because you played backup quarterback on your high school team 24 years ago? Or would someone consider you a chef because you put together a fancy 5-course meal for your girlfriend last summer? I hope the answer is no because identity isn't fixed. If you're not actively using, you're not an addict—you're a person in recovery. I am no longer living that life. I am no longer defined by those choices.

This isn't semantics. Words shape reality. Yes, the risk of relapse lingers, but sobriety isn't about white-knuckling through temptation. Does that mean I am immune to relapse? No. I will never test my resolve by dabbling, but the key difference is this: substances, people, and behaviors no longer hold power over me. My life is not about resisting temptation. It's about actively choosing something greater.

And yet, if the only goal is simply not partaking in a substance, we are missing the bigger picture. Recovery is not just about abstinence—it's about transformation.

Many personal development books talk about the four stages of existence: 1. Survival, 2. Sacrifice, 3. Success, and 4. Significance. Recovery mirrors this progression. Abstinence alone won't catapult you to significance. Abstinence alone does not deliver a life beyond our wildest dreams. But every conscious action that moves us further from who we used to be brings us closer to who we were meant to become.

Passion. Growth. Connection. These things come when we shift our attention toward them. If the *why* is powerful enough, the *how* becomes easier.

That word—significance—means something different to all of us. It may start as a dream, a degree, a relationship, or a certain status. And when those things are lost or derailed, depression and darkness creep in. The urge to numb it all becomes overwhelming.

But today, I challenge you to choose differently. Choose light. Choose love. Choose joy. Choose *them*—your family, your friends, the people who matter. Every single day you do, you move closer to alignment with yourself and the beauty within you, free from addiction.

The journey of recovery is not about what you gain or lose—it's about who you become.

One day, our lives will no longer be measured by time—by hours, days, or years. These things will slip into irrelevance. What will remain are only two things: 1. Memories made and 2. Moments missed. My prayer for you? Let the first category dwarf the second. My hope and desire for everyone reading these words is that they take this to heart. That when your final moments arrive, your memories far outweigh your regrets. That your life is rich with presence, purpose, and participation.

Every morning, you're handed a script. The old version starred Addiction—a tyrant who demanded your everything. The new script? It's blank. You write the lines. So, choose light over numbness. Choose love over fear. Each choice etches you further from who you were and closer to who you're meant to be. This isn't an ending. It's a start.

Welcome to the rest of your days. Welcome to the next chapter of this beautiful, extraordinary gift called life. Lights. Camera. Action. **The beginning!**

The following few pages have been left blank intentionally with the idea that putting pen to paper, just like I did, may help you heal.

Again, there is no magic formula, but each time you write someone or something down, its power is stripped away just a bit more. Let's start with...

1. What are some behaviors that don't need to be part of your future?

2. Write down a list of people, places, and things that no longer serve you on a regular basis.

3. What are some fears, angers, and resentments that you don't have to carry around any longer? (Be specific and honest with yourself. We all have them!)

4. Put a vision of your future that you see for yourself that may only be separated by the obstacles from a few pages earlier. Be clear with how you see the best version of yourself.

5. Spell out some specific goals that you can put into practice immediately and maybe a few that could take a little time.

6. List the people and behaviors you want to be on your new bus in life. What are their roles? Where can you find them or others like them? Who can hold you accountable with the love you deserve?

7. Who do you need to forgive? Who hurt you? How can healing take place now that you are surrounded by care and compassion?

8. Make a gratitude list. What do you have to be grateful for today? Where anxiety or fear exists, joy, peace, and thankfulness are void. Shift your thoughts to what is good and beautiful in your life, and take time daily to consider those blessings we often take for granted.

To My New Friends

Thanks for letting me share my journey from darkness to light with you. The greatest hope that I have in writing "Addict No More" is to give one person the strength to win their personal battle.

To the family who may be simply supportive on this path, know that the biggest gift you can give is love. Nothing can be undone, forgotten, or made up for. The goal is healing that is done "honestly and unpacking."

To those in the middle of the storm, remember all pain, frustration, anger, and sadness is temporary. Tomorrow's fight is for tomorrow. Deal with what's right in front of you today.

The beauty with change is that it keeps happening for everyone. A mindful choice today could impact lives days, months or even years from now. Be that difference.

I would also love to hear from you about any stories of victory, or thoughts/concerns you may have.

Please email me at any time of day or night. TracyAntherc@gmail or let's connect on all socials using my name, Tracy Antherc.

I look forward to connecting with all of you. From this day forward I consider you a friend and I care about my friends.

Love & Respect
Tracy Antherc

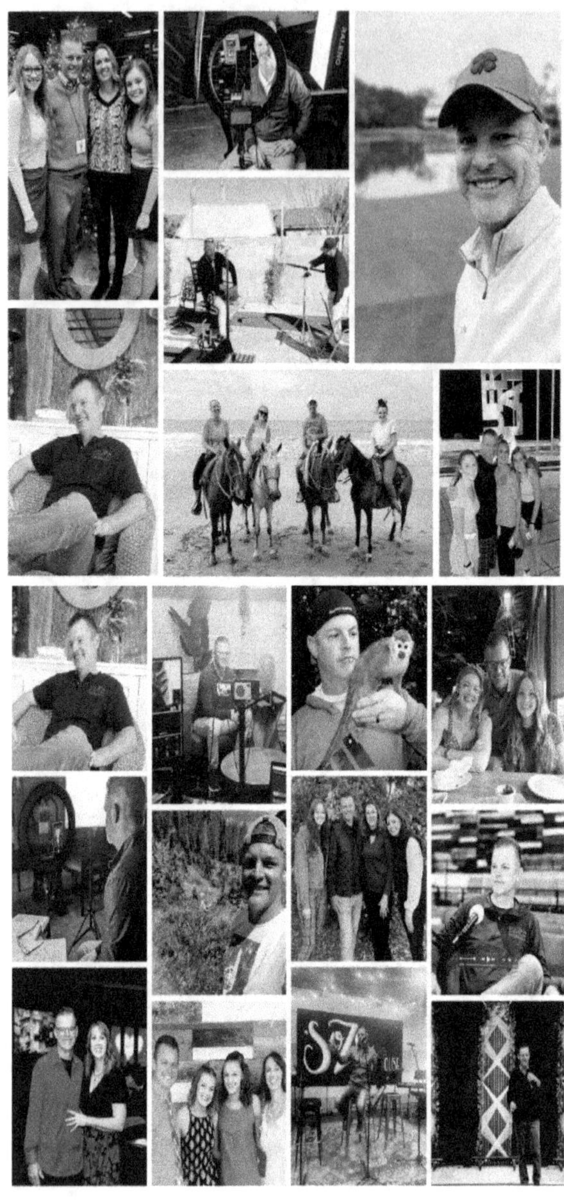